ABOUT THE AUTHOR

Maggie Allder was born and brought up in Gamlingay in Cambridgeshire, the second daughter of a village police officer. She studied at King Alfred's College, Winchester (now the University of Winchester), in Richmond, Virginia, and later at Reading University. She taught for thirty-six years in a Hampshire comprehensive school. After exploring more orthodox forms of Christianity, Maggie became a Quaker, and is happy and settled in the Quaker community in Winchester. She has previously written three novels which form a trilogy of sorts: *Courting Rendition*, *Living with the Leopard* and *A Vision Softly Creeping*. Her fourth and fifth novels, *The Song of the Lost Boy,* and *Beyond the Water Meadows*, both stand alone. All these first five novels take place in and around Winchester, where Maggie still lives. This is the fourth book in her *'Lonely Island'* series following *Dark Waters*, *Marigold's Tale* and *The Reclamation of Jarvis*. Maggie volunteers for a not-for-profit organisation, Human Writes, which aims to provide friendship to prisoners on death row in the USA, and is involved in a small Quaker-run project providing accommodation for those at risk of homelessness in her home city.

HOT, HOT SUMMER

BOOK FOUR OF THE LONELY ISLAND SERIES

MAGGIE ALLDER

Copyright © 2024 Maggie Allder

The moral right of the author has been asserted.

Apart from any fair dealing for the purposes of research or private study, or criticism or review, as permitted under the Copyright, Designs and Patents Act 1988, this publication may only be reproduced, stored or transmitted, in any form or by any means, with the prior permission in writing of the publishers, or in the case of reprographic reproduction in accordance with the terms of licences issued by the Copyright Licensing Agency. Enquiries concerning reproduction outside those terms should be sent to the publishers.

This is a work of fiction. Names, characters, businesses, places, events and incidents are either the products of the author's imagination or used in a fictitious manner. Any resemblance to actual persons, living or dead, or actual events is purely coincidental.

Troubador Publishing Ltd
Unit E2 Airfield Business Park,
Harrison Road, Market Harborough,
Leicestershire. LE16 7UL
Tel: 0116 2792299
Email: books@troubador.co.uk
Web: www.troubador.co.uk

ISBN 978 1836280 231

British Library Cataloguing in Publication Data.
A catalogue record for this book is available from the British Library.

Printed and bound in Great Britain by 4edge Limited
Typeset in 11pt Aldine401 BT by Troubador Publishing Ltd, Leicester, UK

Matador is an imprint of Troubador Publishing Ltd

To refugees everywhere,
and to all who work to improve their lot.

For thou hast been a strength to the poor, a strength to the needy in his distress, a refuge from the storm, a shadow from the heat, when the blast of the terrible ones is as a storm against the wall.

Isaiah 25:4

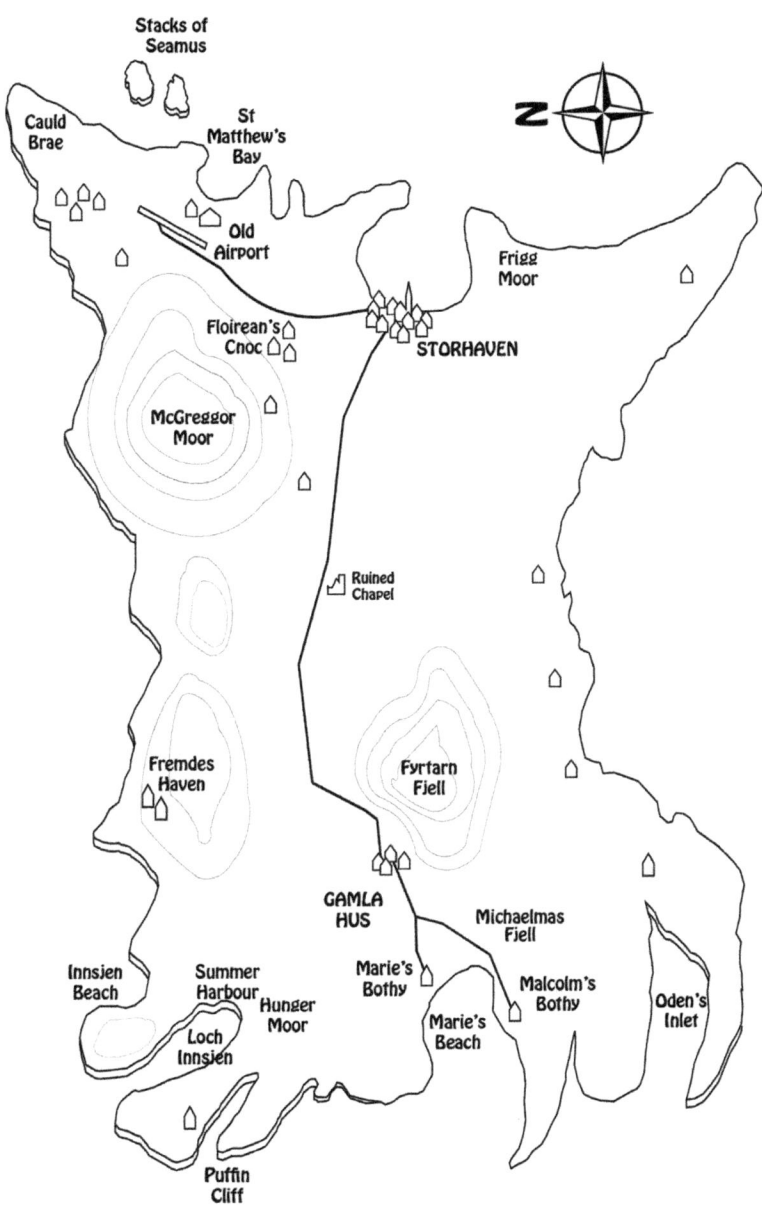

PROLOGUE

There are various ways of climbing Fyrtarn Fjell, the highest mountain on the lonely island of En-Somi. From the summer harbour, which only the *bondii* in the little village of Gamla Hus use, it is pretty hard work whichever way you go. You can follow the path up to Hus, then clamber up the steep side of the fjell, as villagers tend to do at Solstice. Or, if you are coming from the tiny settlement of Fremdes Haven, you need only follow the ridge south-west, which is relatively easy-going, until you reach the track that takes you up the north slope of Fyrtarn. After that, the way can be treacherous in stormy weather unless you know the *fjell* well. Of course, there are other ways of reaching the summit. Jamie MacLoughlan and his family use the track that their children walked every weekday to the school in the village until they reach the burn, and then they veer off to the east and climb over the rocks which are supposed to be a deserted home of the *huldufolk* or little people, although some say they still live there, staying hidden. The island recluse, Jarvis, seems to have discovered other ways to the top. Although at the time of the story I'm telling you now, he was still a relative newcomer, he probably knew the island's wild places better than anyone even then. My partner, Malcolm, and I are not the only ones to have been surprised by his appearance on the summit when we thought we were entirely alone.

People – experts on the mainland – say that Fyrtarn Fjell is important for ancient, pre-Christian reasons. They say that our ancestors believed in a deity who lived in the sky, and that the closer to the heavens you got, the closer to God you were. Personally, I think that's nonsense. Our ancestors weren't stupid! They knew how important the sun is, especially living, as we do, so far to the north, and the *fjell* is the highest point for spotting the sunrise. Or the sunset, of course.

I have thought that our spiritual lives are a little like this. Some people have to start right at the bottom, way down by the metaphorical summer harbour, and then their path will be long, and will involve some steep climbing. Others start on top of the cliffs, like the folk of Fremdes Haven. They will have a few difficult moments as they strive to reach the peak, but a good part of their journey will follow a ridge which is relatively easy-going, and includes some stunning views. Some, like the MacLoughlans, seem to walk their spiritual paths together, helping the weaker ones along the way; and others, like Jarvis, manage alone.

You would have thought that Elin might have had an easy time of it. From early in her childhood, her musical ability was evident, but it was more than that. She had a natural affinity with our bard, Olaf, and he had taken her under his wing and taught her the songs and the music of our island, so that by the time she was eight or nine it was generally accepted that she would become our next keeper of songs and island poet. More than any other of our island bairns, her future seemed secure and her status established. Thinking of the geography of our island, she seemed to be like one of the *bondii* who lived over in Fremdes Haven, in that, spiritually speaking, she would be able to walk the ridge and experience the views, and not struggle too much with harsh conditions. It just shows that you cannot tell.

This is the story of Elin, as I saw it and as it was reported to me by others.

CHAPTER 1

You might already know a bit about our island. Some students made a documentary about us which, we were told, was well received and reached a huge audience worldwide, but that was years ago, and I don't know if people still view it. At around the same time there was quite a lot of press coverage. Climate change was, of course, already a huge issue, but governments were still trying to cope with the fallout; they hadn't given up yet. Some were even denying the seriousness of the problem. A group of climate refugees from south of the border had been dumped on En-Somi to make a fresh start in life.

The consequences were more or less predictable: the refugees didn't have the skills to survive on a tiny island in the wild North Atlantic. They were vulnerable, and there were those ready to take advantage of them. Some were taken off the island again, but others became slaves to a group of unprincipled entrepreneurs who managed to keep their presence on the island more or less a secret for years while they used the labour of the newcomers to do the mechanical and routine work of assembling war drones, the parts for which were made in a workshop we all thought was disused, above the little town of Storhaven. Goodness knows how long the situation might have continued. They were housed over in the old airport – it's a complete ruin now, but the redundant arrivals and departures hall was still standing back in those days.

Then, one night, one of their children was dragged out to sea in a storm, and her little body, barely still alive, was washed up on the beach by my bothy. Naturally, she didn't survive, but her appearance led by stages to the discovery of the small enslaved community. It was the arrest of those heartless entrepreneurs that led to the press coverage – and their trials, of course. Although, I should tell you, if you weren't aware of these events at the time, that the slavers got away with very light sentences. They must have given generously to political parties, we concluded. How else could anyone explain how kindly they were treated by the Crown Office and Procurator Fiscal Service?

For a couple of years after that, life on En-Somi was very eventful. Against the wishes of the *harkrav*, the wealthy elites on the island, we were able to settle the refugees among us. Mostly we achieved this by renovating ruined bothies, which, in itself, was quite demanding. En-Somi had never had mains electricity the way the Shetlands, south of us, had. We had skipped from using peat fires and driftwood with fish-oil lamps to light our homes at night, straight to wind turbines, storage batteries, and ground source heat pumps, but that sort of technology isn't easy to install, and it can be expensive. Still, within a couple of years most of those refugees were in homes of their own, their children were in school, and real friendships had been formed between the refugees and the *bondii* – the common people of the island.

But if you think this sounds like a story with a happy ending, perhaps you need to think again. Do stories ever really have happy endings? In fact, do they ever have endings at all? Over on the west of the island, in Gamla Hus and on the moors surrounding the village, we experienced a fair amount of unity. Everyone seemed to agree that the wee school benefited from having more students, and it was at about the same time that we were able to start building our little community hall. If you look at the island on Google Maps, it's the building on the southern edge of the village. Look for the place where two tracks cross. Right on the crossroads is the village shop; then, as you head towards Fyrtarn Fjell, there's a small bothy. That's where Rose and Si Stewart still live. Then there's a longer building with a turf roof. We won a grant to build it, and it's used for all sorts of events when the schoolroom or the *fi'ilsted* (which you would probably call a pub) are not quite appropriate.

Over in Storhaven, though, things didn't go quite so smoothly. Storhaven is the ferry port, although nowadays – all these years later – we no longer have regular ferries. The storms and the generally unpredictable weather put a stop to schedules. The Storhaven community was much more mixed than our wee village community. For one thing, there were *harkrav* living out in the area known as Floirean's Cnoc. (There still are, by the way!) The *harkrav*, as I mentioned before, are the wealthy elite on the island. There are not that many of them, but they have traditionally had quite a disproportionate degree of power. Then there were those *bondii* who never could accept the refugees. During the first couple of years after the enslavement of the strangers came to light, a split had developed over in Storhaven, with those who were happy to welcome the newcomers frequenting The Old Castle *fi'ilsted*, and those who wanted them gone, meeting at The Vikings' Rest. After a while, though, things settled down, and I suppose we all thought that life was going back to normal.

Those were happy years for me. Malcolm and I had got together soon after he returned to En-Somi, the island of his birth. The ever-more-violent storms prevented our island bairns from going to Shetland for school as they had done in the past, and they started to use distance learning. I loved having my son Duncan at home. In a changing and dangerous world, most island families preferred to keep their kin close. We were all becoming more and more self-sufficient, but back then we could still order goods from the mainland and they usually arrived sooner or later.

I wouldn't say that life was easy. We were (and still are) basically crofters, and a crofter's life is demanding, but we were sheltered from so much that was making life ever harder for those in more populated places. Malcolm's bairns, grown up and living across the water, told us of sudden and unexpected food shortages. Suddenly there would be no bread, or milk would become unobtainable. People started to eat less meat. Supplies of medication unexpectedly ran short, and there were regular power cuts. Moira, Malcolm's sister, was twice flooded out of her Glasgow home and moved to join her son in Blair Athol on the edge of the Cairngorms National Park, which was bleak in the winter, but a good place to live if you were a whisky lover! I suppose, having always been relatively self-sufficient, we were better equipped than most to survive the terrible effects of climate change.

Several years passed without incident. Well, of course that isn't true! For Verity and Lyle, close friends with Malcolm and me, the birth of their second child in the middle of the night during a hurricane was definitely memorable! And to our surprise, Rose and Si had another child. There was no reason they shouldn't – they were still relatively young – but Rose's previous childbirths had not been easy, and Thistle was barely two when wee Alec came into the world. Si was ridiculously proud of his son, and Rose put on a little weight and didn't lose it, and took on that look that some mothers have, of contentment mixed with harassment!

The elections to the *Oyrod*, the island council, were hardly uneventful either. For two years we had struggled with land-use taxes imposed to cover the costs incurred by the arrival of the refugees in our community. It was true that we needed more supplies in the schools, but the *bondii* believed that a lot of the increased and necessary expenditure on our small rocky island was the result of the changing weather conditions, not the advent of the newcomers. For the first time we employed a doctor, who arrived in Storhaven and settled into the flat that used to be Verity's when she was a minister of the only kirk on the island.

The new doctor caused quite a stir, but that's another story. The fact is that we needed to have medical help on En-Somi because the storms made it so difficult for helicopters to come over from Shetland in emergencies. It was nothing to do with the refugees, although I'm sure that the fact of Dr Emmylou coming over from Storhaven when wee Alec was born was the reason that Rose, once a refugee and a slave, had the first straightforward birth of her life!

All those things happened in what seemed to be the ordinary run of En-Somi life. The elections to the *Oyrod*, which I was about to tell you about, felt much more exceptional. There had often been one or two *bondii* on that committee. Holti, the old man who lived over in Caldbrae with young Mo and Quincy, had become quite an activist, and Malcolm's friend, Ingrid, did what she could, but the *harkrav* always held the balance of power. Well, that is, until the elections. This must have been two or three years after the discovery of the refugees and a bit before the story I'm going to tell you now. When the land taxes were raised, we realised that something had to be done; that we *bondii* needed better representation on the island council. Campaigning started almost as soon as those crippling tax demands started to arrive at our bothies. Petter and Malcolm led the charge, so to speak, on our side of En-Somi, and Malcolm was asked to stand for office by common consent. It made matters a little easier that Blair Munro, our previous representative, had left the island in disgrace. None of us knew why he hadn't been prosecuted for theft, but that is the way of things if you are *harkrav* with friends in high places!

I remember the day the results came through. We voted online using some absurdly complicated forms and then we had to wait for the electoral commission in Aberdeen to count the votes and give us the results. Although we all knew – or, anyhow, believed – that Malcolm would win easily, we weren't completely sure that somewhere along the line there might not be some foul play. A lot of us had gathered at the *fi'ilsted*, phones and tablets turned on, awaiting the publication of the results. They should have been out by 4 o'clock and Petter had a bottle of his best whisky behind the bar, ready for the celebrations. We waited and waited, but no results pinged onto our screens.

"I'll call Aberdeen," offered Lyle. Being the local *nasyoni* or police officer, he had an official phone and wouldn't have to pay the newly-imposed tariff for long-distance calls. He came back just a few minutes later. "I couldn't really get any sense out of them," he told us. "They said there was a hitch in proceedings."

"A hitch in proceedings?" Yanni was indignant. "How could there be? It was a pretty straightforward process – once we had mastered those ridiculous forms!"

"Probably *harkrav* interference," offered Robert, rather gloomily.

"Will you be able to ask for a recount?" Elise wondered. She had left the island briefly to finish her degree, but had just returned, if I remember rightly.

"I don't think I can wait any longer," Si told us. "Supper and bedtimes are hard work now the wee bairn is on the scene. Two children under three!" He sounded as proud as punch. "Rose needs all the help I can give her!"

Soon after that, others started to leave. It was May, or round about that time anyhow, and there were several hours of daylight left for work to be done around our bothies. Malcolm and I headed back to my place, where my son, Duncan, should have been studying with his friend, Alana.

In fact, the results weren't declared until after 9 o'clock. I had come in from my small vegetable patch and Malcolm had put in a couple of hours' fishing. We were sitting round the small table which served as a dining table and a desk at different times of the day. The bothy door was open. The sun hadn't quite set, but on our side of the island it was already shadowy because of the hills to our east. We could hear the waves breaking on the beach and the shrill, grating call of the Arctic terns guarding their nests. Carried on the wind was the trilling of the ground-nesting curlews which we knew were on the high moorland north of my bothy. There was an occasional creaking sound from my wind turbine as it lazily turned in the breeze, and the gentle baaing of sheep, grazing all around. It was a peaceful time of day.

Duncan stretched, and reached out for his phone, which he was not allowed to have at the table while we ate. "Hey! The results are in!" he exclaimed.

Both Malcolm and I dived for our phones, but even before we were able to reach the right site, they started to ping. From all across the west of En-Somi friends were sending messages of congratulation. Malcolm was our newly elected representative. Several other *bondii* had been elected too, giving us, for the first time ever, the balance of power on the council. A narrow balance of power, though: five *harkrav* and six *bondii*.

We didn't consume Petter's good celebratory whisky until a couple of days later, but we did open our own home brew, and I remember that Duncan, who must have been nearly fourteen by then, had his share.

★★★

I think it was after that, probably the next summer, that we opened the meeting house. The grant people based on the Isle of Mann had been a joy to work with, although they never managed to come over in person. Twice they planned to visit, but on both occasions the weather prevented their travel. Elise made a video of the construction of the building – or, rather, its renovation – and included the opening ceremony to show our Manx benefactors the fruit of their generosity.

Quite a crowd of us gathered for the occasion. Petter had volunteered to provide a bottle of something to break against the door as if we were launching a ship. We had done something similar when Si and Rose first moved into their bothy. However, it had already been agreed that, among its many uses, the meeting house was to be the place where Quaker meetings were to be held on Sundays. I think it was always understood, too, that the building would never serve alcohol, because the *fi'ilsted* was just a stone's throw away, and under no circumstances did anyone want to take trade away from Petter and Malchi. Instead, we tied a ribbon across the door and Malcolm, as our *Oyrod* representative, cut it with great ceremony and we all gathered inside to eat kale pasties and drink tea.

It is difficult now to remember how we managed without the meeting house. Back then, Sunday worship was a very minor part of its use. Sometimes only Verity, Malcolm and I gathered, and none of us were officially Quakers. It was only later that others started to join us. We would have been astounded back then, if we had been able to look into the future and see so many people trudging through gales, sleet and snow to join in silent worship!

In those days, the main use of the building was as a centre for our teenagers. They were all involved in distance learning – there were not enough of them to form a class and, as I have mentioned before, parents were reluctant to allow their bairns to go to Shetland when we never knew when or how they might return. They studied at home – or, as often as not, in the homes of their friends – but they tended to meet at the meeting house most weekday afternoons. Some needed to collect younger siblings from Sigrid's classes, but others just liked the companionship. They took their summer examinations there too.

I think it is fair to say that those were comfortable years. Despite the chaos in the world, the very many 'natural' disasters (which we all knew were not natural at all), the wars, and the rumours of wars, we could still see a future for ourselves and our children.

CHAPTER 2

I remember when I first became aware that all might not be well with wee Elin. The day started normally enough. Once again it was summer, almost an anniversary of the *Oyrod* elections. Malcolm had a few tasks to do for the council, and I had been hanging bunches of herbs on a line in the kitchen area, to dry. The door to our bothy was open, and a pleasant breeze cooled the air so that the bairns, dressed in shorts and T-shirts, were comfortable. Duncan and Alana had been helping Marigold with her Norwegian. At seventeen they were both fairly fluent, but fifteen-year-old Marigold was pretty good too. She had a way with languages. On an everyday basis she spoke exactly like the other En-Somi teenagers, complete with a smattering of dialect and a few words gleaned from online games originating from far afield. At home, though, or if she was visiting our resident hermit, Jarvis, she still sounded like the wee lassie I had first got to know years earlier, complete with dropped Hs and an F sound instead of TH. Having finished with the herbs, I had been lying on my bed up on the sleeping platform, half-reading and half-listening to the four teenagers and feeling a little surprised, as I often was by then, at how grown-up they had become.

"Paps would love the way you said that!" Duncan was telling Marigold. "You sound just like my Norwegian half-sisters! Paps still sounds like a Scot – or, at least, like someone from En-Somi!" He sounded as if he were smiling. "So do you, Alana!"

"I don't have the ear for it," remarked Alana, not seeming at all put out.

"And you don't spend much time on it," Andy added. He was still a slight, pale lad, but tall, and with a voice as deep as his father's. "Duncan talks to his paps and that crowd all the time, so he gets masses of practice."

"Well, that's true," remarked Duncan. "I need to be good at Norwegian. I'm half-hoping to go to university there."

Marigold chipped in. "Do you realise," she pointed out, "that I have never left this island?" She sounded thoughtful. "I'm not sure I ever want to."

"*Nei.*" Andy was in complete agreement. "Nor do I! Mam used to take me over to Shetland when I was a bairn, and twice to Edinburgh to see specialists, but I was always glad to get home." He chuckled. "Everywhere is 'abroad' to me!"

"But we don't meet many people here," Duncan pointed out. "If I go to Tromsø I'll meet all sorts – different nationalities, different experiences…"

"*Aja.*" Alana was interested in human rights; in justice and inequality. She was playing with ideas for her career as a lawyer, or maybe working for one of those NGOs that had nearly been banned by the Westminster government a few years earlier. "There's a limit to how much we can contribute to the world living here."

Marigold, as always, was interested in Alana's comment. Apparently, the notion of trying to do something significant to contribute to the wider world was a new idea to her. "Do you think we have to achieve something big to do our bit for society?" she queried. "I mean – well, Marie and Malcolm contributed quite a lot when they freed us, and they didn't leave the island to do that! And now Malcolm's contributing by being on the *Oyrod.*"

"*Aja,*" Andy agreed. "And look how much Malchi contributes by cooking all those wonderful meals!"

Typical teenagers! I thought. *Sooner or later, the subject always comes round to food!*

"Are you bairns staying for dinner?" I called, peering over the edge of the sleeping platform. "Because I warn you, if you are, there'll be a pile of potatoes to peel!"

***

Andy hadn't stayed, I remember, because he was feeling weary. There was something amiss with the lad all through his childhood and it seemed to me that he had used up all his strength in growing taller. I knew that his parents, Alf and Fiona, were worried. Alana decided to walk up to the village with him, (she was concerned in case he became unwell when he was out on the moors alone), so only Duncan and Marigold ate with us.

"You know," Marigold told us, putting her spoon neatly into her empty soup bowl, "when I first went to the school, when everything was so new, it seemed to me as if all the island bairns were alike. You know – some were boys and some were girls, and some were older than others, but they all spoke the same, they said the same sorts of things and – I don't know! They all seemed so similar to each other and so different from me! But now everyone I know is such an individual."

"*Aja*," agreed Duncan with his mouth full. "It's strange. When I was in school in Lerwick and first met those twins from Foula, I absolutely couldn't tell them apart. But about half a term in, I suddenly realised I knew which was which. They each looked like themselves, and I never muddled them up again." He chuckled at a memory. "Some of the teachers did, though!"

"What made you think of that, Marigold?" Malcolm was serving second helpings.

"All this talk about what we'll do when we finish school," the lass explained. "Alana will go to the mainland and do something big. You want to go to Norway, don't you, Duncan? Andy and I want to stay on the island, but for different reasons…"

"You once told me," Duncan reminded Marigold, "that you wanted to marry Christian when you grew up!"

"Did I?" Marigold laughed. "I was really into people marrying each other for a little while, because I'd been a bridesmaid for Verity. Do you remember? In that pretty pink dress? Wee Thistle plays dressing-up with it now, although it's much too big for her!"

"It looks to me," Duncan went on, "as if young Elin is interested in Christian now."

"Ah, now there's an interesting situation!" Malcolm was sitting back, looking contented. I knew that he loved having these two bairns around. He had raised his own children alone after his wife died, and seen them fly the nest, and now he was enjoying the same thing again.

"Christian can only be fifteen or so," I pointed out. "And Elin's younger. Too young to be thinking of settling down. It'll just be a phase."

"Mm." Malcolm knew that. "But our Elin is no ordinary teenager, is she?"

"*Nei*," Duncan agreed. "She's got a calling!"

"You mean, because she's apprenticed to Olaf? Because she could be the next island bard?" Marigold sounded doubtful.

"*Aja*." Malcolm swilled the water round in his glass. "That's what I meant. If things work out that way, she'll have a very special role in our community. There'll be no leaving En-Somi for her! It would be ideal if she married a local."

"I can't see it," Marigold told us. "I know she's gifted. Goodness, that song she wrote about the children who died when that school roof collapsed on them…"

"'A Lament for the Innocent'," Duncan reminded us.

"*Aja*," the lassie agreed. "It was so beautiful. It had me in tears. But there's more to being the island bard than being able to write wonderful songs, isn't there? Isn't a bard supposed to be wise? I wouldn't say Elin shows much sign of wisdom!"

I was surprised. Marigold didn't miss much, it was true, but she was rarely critical of others. In fact, I reflected, she sounded more scornful than judgemental.

Malcolm was interested. "Why do you say that?" he wanted to know.

Marigold went a little pink. "Well…" She looked away from us, hesitating. "Perhaps I shouldn't have said… She's like two people. She writes these amazing songs, and when she's singing them there's a sort of light around her. But then – you know, she's absolutely boy-mad! That other Elin, the one who sits on Christian's lap and giggles when we're at the meeting house – she just seems… *felbilli*."

I looked at my partner and son. I still heard dialect words that were new to me.

"Common," explained Duncan.

"Cheap," Malcolm added.

"Ah!" I had some sympathy for wee Elin. She was an only child raised by a doting father, and she had always seemed a little different from the other bairns. There were a lot of expectations circling Elin and that couldn't be easy for her, and the pressure to fit in, to belong, can be very strong in a teenager's life. "She won't be the first bairn to be boy-mad on this island! It usually passes."

"*Aja*," Marigold agreed, sounding more worried than critical. "But it isn't the behaviour of an apprenticed bard, is it?"

★★★

A few years before all this – the story of Elin that I'm telling you now – our community in Gamla Hus had established a tradition of eating together regularly. For a while, the majority of us shared a meal most Friday afternoons when lessons at the primary school had finished. It was important that we supported each other both physically and emotionally when our very continuation on the island seemed to be threatened. The habit faded out, if I remember rightly, during the second summer after it started. We could see the end of the high taxation so the need to support each other had faded, and there was work to do on the land and in the sea. Many of us, however, were reluctant to see the custom die out altogether, and so Sigrid (the schoolteacher), Verity and Malchi agreed to organise gatherings, with food provided, on the last day of each school term.

It was a very hot day. You would think, living so far north, that we would never see temperatures above thirty degrees Celsius, but that day in early June it was nearer to thirty-five degrees! The weather was not unexpected. There had been red warnings for huge swathes of Europe and all over the UK for days, and the news bulletins told the tale of deaths from heatstroke and of fires sweeping across moorland and forest. In Gamla Hus there was a steady breeze from the west, which was good news for us. It meant that although we saw the stunning sunsets caused by all the smoke in the atmosphere, the wind smelt fresh; of sea and flowering moorland plants. En-Somi is a very windy island, and the breeze was a godsend to everyone.

Sigrid and Malchi had organised the teenagers to carry the school tables outside. They were placed on the grass where the bairns played and on the track – anywhere in the centre of the village where the land was flat. Petter and Si rigged up a sort of pergola over some of the seating areas using bed sheets, and Malchi prepared a seafood salad which, he informed us proudly, had all been harvested within the last twenty-four hours. Lyle's parents were there, I remember. They were quite elderly by then and Lyle's mam had some sort of mobility issues, so they were only able to come over if someone could let them have the use of a pony, or if an intrepid driver of a trap was willing to risk the primitive track that served Fremdes Haven. Of course, they loved to be in Hus; to see their grandchildren and the friends they had known all their lives. They would stay at the *fi'ilsted* in order to spend time with the wee ones. Lyle's mam, I remember, was hobbling round offering her home-made sunscreen to all the parents. There are altogether too many redheads among us and they burn so easily!

I remember Elise asking for some of the cream as well. "I burn too, you know!" she told us. "It just doesn't show so much!"

It was on that occasion that I saw what Marigold meant about Elin. It was the custom that Olaf and Elin played and sang while we ate, and Petter had brought out a couple of his small, round stools from the *fi'ilsted* for them to sit on. Most of the songs were traditional and known to everyone on En-Somi, and we had all heard the achingly sad 'Lament for the Innocent' before, but there was an instrumental piece which only Elin played. She had a new *langspil* or zither – at least, I hadn't noticed it before – made of dark wood with a complicated Celtic design painted on the board under the strings. She played with a pick in her right hand while her left hand strummed and stroked the accompaniment. It was not a new song, nor was it traditional Scots – I had known it from music shows on the radio in my childhood. Maybe it had been a pop song. I think it was called 'The Sound of Silence', and it was stunningly beautiful. I remember that the whole assembled crowd went quiet as if a spell had been cast. Even wee Alec stopped chattering! When she finished playing, there was a sort of pause. It seemed as if, for a moment, nobody moved or spoke. I could hear the curlews on the moor, and see the gulls, attracted by our food and waiting for us to move away so that they could scavenge. I became suddenly aware that the sun had moved round and my right arm was burning.

Then, quite suddenly, as if from nowhere, came shouting: "Bravo! Bravo!" followed by clapping. And round the corner by the shop came a small group of youths. I recognised one or two of them, vaguely. They were Storhaven lads. I had seen them around the quay when our teenagers used to catch the ferry to school, but of course they had grown since then. Boys who had been rather sweet, naive and polite, looked slightly threatening now in their trendy boaters and wrap-around sunglasses. And there was one boy I didn't think I had ever seen before.

"Uh – oh!" exclaimed Duncan under his breath, beside me.

"Who are they?" asked Malcolm, leaning across to speak quietly to my son.

"I don't know them all," Duncan answered. He was talking to us, but watching the lads as they sauntered down the track towards our feast. "That guy in the red T-shirt, that's Mac MacLoughlan's cousin. A year older than me. Last I heard, he was still on Shetland. And the lad all in black, he's a Stewart, I think. And I might recognise the tall one, a bit older than the others..."

Marigold, who was seated round the corner of the table, leaned across to remind us. "Isn't he the lad who beat up Harris? Don't you remember? We saw him on that video. *Harkrav.*"

The little group of youths stopped at the first table they came to. Malchi and Petter were seated there, with Lyle's parents and a couple of others. The *harkrav* lad – he was more of a young man, really – picked up some leaves from the salad bowl in the middle of the table, and ate them.

"Nice dressing!" he approved in a slightly supercilious voice. "I had heard that even the *bondii* appreciate good food!" He turned to his little gang of admiring friends. "It's not all neeps and potatoes, then!"

They all laughed loudly, although several of them were *bondii* themselves. I could feel Duncan bristling besides me.

Another lad wandered down the track to our table. He looked approvingly at Marigold, who was wearing shorts and a sleeveless blouse and who did look very attractive. "So, bonnie lass!" he said. "What are you doing with these old fogies? Wouldn't you rather come and hang out with us?"

At once Malcolm stood, and so did several men at other tables. Duncan rose to his feet too, fists clenched. Marigold looked confused.

"All right! All right!" the youth said, glancing at the standing men and backing away. "Can't blame a man for liking the look of a sexy girl!"

"The fact is," it was the *harkrav* lad again, "we've come here on an errand. This is barbecue weather and we're going down to the beach by Loch Innsjen. We wondered if any of you would like to come?" The youth looked cheekily at Malcolm, who was still standing. "It's a party for young people, Grandad. You'll have to stay at home, I'm afraid!"

I glanced around at our young people. Duncan was glaring at the lad. Marigold was looking down at her lap. Further down the track, Alana was sitting with her parents, a look of utter scorn on her face. Andy looked, I thought, almost frightened.

The youth glanced towards the rigged-up pergola where Harris and Elise were seated. "And no dusky *sommy klingers* either!" he proclaimed.

Petter stood and took a step towards the small group still gathered near his table. Malcolm went and joined him. Lyle, I noticed, was filming the encounter.

"How very kind of you to pay us a visit!" said Petter. "And so thoughtful of you to think of inviting some of us to your barbecue. However, as you see, we have a celebration of our own going on, so perhaps it would be as well if you left?"

The one lad who had separated himself from his friends, the boy who had approached Marigold, sauntered back between the tables to join his gang. On his way he passed Elin and Olaf, and carelessly ruffled Elin's hair. "Cute!" he said.

The five youths had backed off a little from Petter when Malcolm had joined him, but only by a few feet. In the tense silence that had fallen on our gathering, they just stood there, expressions hidden behind their sunglasses.

Malcolm spoke then. He was as calm as Petter, but his voice had an air of authority I didn't often hear. "Perhaps you didn't understand!" he suggested. "This is a private occasion. Invitation only. And you were not invited. So, this would be the ideal time for you to leave!" Then, when the gang stood their ground, he added firmly, "Now!"

"Oh well, if you're not interested…" said the *harkrav* lad, and turned to leave.

His friends glanced round at us one more time. The boy who had approached our table made a strange clicking sound with his tongue when his eyes lit on Marigold and then on Elin; then they all swivelled on their heels to follow their leader.

"Wait!" It was Elin. She had leapt to her feet, and, leaving her beautiful *langspil* on the stool, she started to follow the intruders. "I'll come!" she called. Then, perhaps realising how much disapproval was emanating from our community, she turned and, looking directly at Olaf, said, "It's only a barbecue! And I love barbecues!"

And with that, she left.

CHAPTER 3

By the following morning Petter had moved half the tables from their various party locations and placed them in a row on the track at the front of the *fi'ilsted* where, for the morning at any rate, they were in the shadow cast by the building, so that people could sit out there in comfort. It rather narrowed the track and made it tricky for Robert, who was taking his pony and cart over to Fremdes Haven with Lyle's parents. Verity and her two bairns were also on board. They managed to squeeze past, although it wasn't easy. I watched in amusement as wee Joel peered over the side of the cart and called out detailed but incorrect instructions: "Right a bit! You're going to hit a rock! Oh, left! Left!" The laddie hadn't quite distinguished his left from his right.

Robert was grinning broadly, and took it all in good part. "Thank you, young Joel!" he exclaimed. "What would I do without you?"

Elin's paps was sitting in the shade at one of the tables outside the *fi'ilsted* with Olaf. Both men looked worried. As I approached, Elin's paps stood to leave. He gave me a little wave and called out, "Don't take it personally, Marie! I want to catch the tide!"

"Join me for tea?" Olaf asked, and on the spur of the moment I agreed, although actually I had been on my way up to the Kullander's place.

Petter came out wearing shorts and flip-flops and offered us both a new pot. "I haven't worn these clothes for two years!" he told us. "Malchi says they make me look younger, but I'm not so sure…"

Olaf smiled at me. "All this concern about how he looks…" he complained, but he was obviously amused. "I remember young Petter as a lad. I used to worry about him. Finding Malchi was the best thing that could have happened for them both – even if Petter's parents could never quite accept it."

I texted Fiona to let her know I'd be late, then put my phone in my back pocket out of the way. "The teenage years seem to be so risky," I agreed.

"Your Duncan seems to have his feet on the ground," Olaf remarked. "And wee Marigold too. A lovely bairn, that one!"

"*Aja*, so far so good," I agreed, "but you never know what'll happen next!"

"*Nei.*" There was a worried frown on Olaf's old, creased face. "Wee Elin arrived home at dawn," he told me. "Her paps was just telling me. She spent all night down on the beach at the head of Loch Innsjen with those laddies. Drinking and who knows what."

I paused for a moment before asking, "Do you know who they are, those bairns? Duncan and Marigold thought that one of the *harkrav* lads was the person who attacked Harris. Do you remember?"

"Oh, *nei*, he isn't," Olaf told me. "The laddie we had the privilege of meeting yesterday is Magnus Munro, Blair's younger bairn. He was at school on the mainland. It was his older brother who assaulted Harris. They're alike in more ways than one, so I'm told."

I wondered, not for the first time, how Olaf knew so much. He rarely used his phone, he wasn't interested in social media, and although he had a radio, Marigold had once told me that he hardly ever listened to it. "A night on the beach won't be the end of the world," I comforted Olaf, although I felt a wee bit hypocritical. How would I feel if it had been Marigold who had left with that little gang? Or even Duncan?"

"*Nei,*" agreed Olaf, although he didn't sound convinced. "The bairn needs to find her own way... It's just that..." He reached out and held my hand across the table. "It's just that we think we've driven her too hard, maybe. Her paps and me. Her gifts are so obvious, and she seemed so keen to learn, and so happy... Even a month ago, when I handed her that new *langspil* as a thirteenth birthday present, she seemed so delighted. But you saw her yesterday evening. She just put it down and walked away..."

"It's a difficult age," I said again, "and she's grown up without her mam..."

"I'm frightened," Olaf confessed. He let go of my hand. "She's... Despite the best efforts of her paps and me, she seems unprotected, that lassie. Her mam was the same. She's so sensitive, as if she's missing some sort of emotional protective covering, and a little lost, with no woman to turn to, to mother her... And I'm confused. The way ahead doesn't seem so clear – I've taken too much for granted. If Elin isn't going to be the new bard, who will be? I've always believed... I thought I had seen that it was to be Elin. I haven't looked any further; not considered any other possibilities... But last night... Until then I was so sure... And now I'm wondering if I only saw what I wanted to see. Is there another side to our wee Elin that might make her unsuitable?"

I had never seen the old man look so vulnerable or so unhappy. What could I say? One night on a beach with a crowd of Storhaven lads didn't seem to me to be so terrible. The wee lass needed to be a teenager before she could be an adult, taking on all the responsibilities of a bard. Weren't Olaf and Elin's paps overreacting? "We'll think of her in our Sunday meeting," I told him, although it sounded a bit lame to me. "Before then, of course, but especially on Sunday."

"Thank you." He smiled then, looking more like his old self. "It's easy to think that it's all up to me. What did the Greeks call it? Hubris? If we're to have a new bard, we're to have a new bard, and if not... I ought to have a little more faith in the universe, or that Spirit you seek in your meetings!" The old man sat back in his chair. "Anyhow, you didn't come here to listen to me! What does your day hold, young Marie?"

So, I told him about our plan for making blaeberry jam, and how we had to be so careful with our glass jars now that they had become so difficult to replace, and about how much fun Fiona, Frankie and wee Shirley had had the previous Sunday, collecting the black fruit. Olaf smiled, and recalled his own mam doing the same when he was a bairn over on Hunger Moor. Then I left to climb the path to the Kullander's place, and Olaf took his stick and headed up the track towards the crossroads.

It must have looked as if all was well, but I had a sort of ache within me, a nagging feeling somewhere close to my heart, that was telling me that, actually, all was not well at all.

★★★

It was about then that Elise's parents came over to visit. From the time, several years earlier, that Elise had been one of three students making that documentary to submit as part of their final degrees, the lassie had seemed at home among us. After a couple of months, she had gone back to Edinburgh to continue her course, but she had been back and forth ever since. I heard from Harris that she had done really well in the end, even if her degree did take her longer than anticipated because of her frequent sojourns with us. Harris was living in Malcolm's bothy by then since Malcolm lived permanently in mine, and when Elise at last returned to the island for good, she had moved in with him.

Her parents were to arrive by helicopter from Shetland. They had wanted to book a ferry passage because it would be environmentally friendlier, but the ferry company no longer took bookings in advance. They could never predict when the boat would be able to make the crossing. Their helicopter was to land at the old airport, and Harris had asked to borrow Malcolm's ponies and trap to meet them.

I was a little anxious about the visit. "They'll find us very unsophisticated," I suggested to Malcolm. "And they haven't met Harris before. He's a bit… alternative!"

It was evening, and we were sitting in front of my bothy, looking out to sea. The heat had subsided a little as the sun set, but a sort of warmth hung heavily in the air. The breeze had dropped and midges had suddenly appeared everywhere, so that, in our shorts and T-shirts, we were constantly itchy.

"I can see why Americans put screens on their porches," Malcolm commented, scratching his leg. "If only our wonderful En-Somi wind would start blowing again!"

"But at least Elise's parents will be able to get here," I pointed out. "I wonder if Harris is nervous?"

"We're talking about the people who raised Elise," Malcolm pointed out. "They can't have raised a lassie like her if they're *harkrav* – or the mainland equivalent!"

"Well, *nei*, but you know…"

I need not have worried. In the middle of the following afternoon, while I was sitting on my beach, knitting and watching Malcolm fishing from his little boat just beyond the rocky outcrop, my phone pinged. It was a message and a photograph from Elise. Three people were standing in front of the ruined airport. The middle one was Elise; on one side stood a tall, dark man with white hair, and on the other a woman who bore such a likeness to Elise that it almost took my breath away. 'Safely arrived!' the lassie had texted. 'Come for tea tomorrow morning?' Her parents, dressed in jeans and appearing slightly windswept, didn't look remotely like *harkrav*.

***

In fact, they were, as I might have guessed, charming. When Malcolm and I arrived at his bothy they were sitting outside on the stone bench (which I could still remember being built) and drinking iced dandelion tea from tall wooden beakers. Elise's mam was wearing a pretty, loose dress, and she had bare feet. Her paps sported an unbuttoned shirt. We could hear their laughter even before we rounded the side of the bothy. We knew that they were professional people. Elise had told me that her paps was a doctor. She hadn't mentioned that he was a leading expert in medical genetics and I didn't find out that morning. Her mother seemed to be an ordinary, kind and cheerful woman, although she, too, held a position of some dignity in the counselling world.

I'm not sure now, looking back, why I feared that Elise's parents might consider themselves better than us. After all, we had professional people among those who still counted as *bondii* on the island. Malcolm, when all was said and done, had been a social worker; Sigrid was a fully qualified teacher and her daughter had an accountancy degree from Aberdeen. Perhaps the events of the past five years, the bad feeling between *harkrav* and *bondii,* had made me feel unsettled; a little more aware of status than is really healthy.

Anyhow, Elise's parents stayed for two weeks and we had a lot of fun. Malcolm took Elise's paps fishing, and Harris and Elise took them over to visit Harris's parents. I would have loved to see how that worked out, knowing as we all did that Harris's paps had been disappointed in his son. Harris had dropped out of university some years earlier. I wondered whether the appearance of Elise, from such an obviously successful family, might make things better. Or might they worry about their very different cultural backgrounds?

One evening we all went over to Innsjen Beach. It is the best accessible beach on our side of En-Somi, with a wide stretch of light golden sand and a little burn that empties out, gurgling, from the moor. It is north-facing and the currents around the island seem to work in such a way that, unlike my beach, very little is washed up on the shore. It can be extraordinarily bleak in wintertime, with winds whistling over the sand and stinging the face of anyone intrepid enough to walk there. But in the summer, it can be wonderful; the waves rolling lazily in; the sea glinting and sparkling. More often than not, the *bondii* on our side of the island celebrate the Summer Solstice with a picnic there, with various swimming and boating competitions, and it was not unusual for folk from more distant parts of En-Somi to come too.

That afternoon, I remember, we were joined by several other members of our community. Si and Rose were there with their two youngest, and Duncan, Marigold, Andy and Alana had dug a barbecue pit. The youngsters swam and Malcolm and I joined them although the sea was bitingly cold, and Elise's mam paddled in the surf and laughed about how chilly it was. We ate lamb kebabs and wee Thistle and Alec slept on towels at the foot of the dunes. Down on the beach there was a steady breeze, and despite the lingering heat, we were comfortable. Malcolm was experimenting with brewing our own alcoholic drinks that summer – it was getting harder and harder to import anything – and we had a cask of his newly fermented beer with us as well as the usual dandelion tea. I remember seeing Marigold sitting a little distance from the fire, talking earnestly with Elise's mother. Si, Harris and Elise's paps were walking along the shoreline. They had been collecting driftwood at first, (rather unsuccessfully because it's not a good beach for gleaning), but later they seemed to be in deep conversation, and every now and again a chuckle or a roar of laughter reached us from the three men. It was a lovely, peaceful evening. Until –

"Malcolm!" It was Harris calling.

Malcolm stretched lazily and rose to his feet. "Have you found something interesting?" he called as he strolled towards them. "Marigold once found a small leather purse with an American dollar coin in it! But that was on Marie's beach…"

He joined the small group. Harris was holding something and they were all peering at it in the low, slanting light of the evening. There was a little subdued conversation, then the four returned to the rest of us. Elise's father was looking grave. Harris and Malcolm were visibly worried. Si had turned a deathly white.

"What have you found?" I asked.

Silently, Harris held out the object in his hand. I had no idea what I was looking at. It was a small clear plastic container of the sort that, decades earlier, people on the mainland used to deliver Indian takeaway meals. One corner of it was covered in sand, but the part of the lid that had been washed clean by the sea was almost transparent. Inside I could see something yellowy-brown; organic-looking.

"Mushrooms?" I asked, thinking that it made no sense.

"*Aja*." Harris sounded grim. "Half buried, right at the water's edge."

"Washed in by the tide, maybe?" I still hadn't realised why the others were looking so grim.

"Do you have a drug problem on the island?" It was the first time I had heard Elise's paps use such a professional voice.

"*Nei!*" I exclaimed.

But at the same time, Harris replied, "Maybe."

Malcolm turned to me. "They look like magic mushrooms," he told me. "Hallucinogenic drugs. Easy enough to grow, if you know what you're doing."

"But, on En-Somi?" It seemed almost ridiculous to me. We saw films on streaming services about armed police officers taking down drug traffickers in decaying American cities, and appeals for donations for worthy charities running rehabilitation centres in our big conurbations on the mainland, but here? On this lonely island? Hallucinogenics?

We all looked at each other in the gathering gloom.

"They must have been washed ashore from somewhere else!" I suggested. "Shetland, maybe? Or Iceland? The Faroes?"

"It's not likely," Harris responded.

"But this is where we bring our kids to play!" Si looked really upset. "I thought it was a safe place! And Sigrid brings her classes down here. I thought we had got away from this sort of thing..."

We were all quiet, looking at the plastic container as if it might give us a clue about the origin of its contents.

Then, "You know who else comes here, to this beach?" Malcolm asked, speaking thoughtfully.

Then I realised. "*Aja*," I answered. "That Munro boy and his gang." I didn't say it, but I was thinking, *And Elin.*

CHAPTER 4

The weather was changing. Further south there had been massive thunderstorms, with impressive footage of lightning shown on the news and pictures of streams and rivers tearing through communities carrying fallen trees and whirling debris. We woke up on the morning after the barbecue to the sight of heavy, dark clouds to the south, although the sea to the west, as I looked out from my window, still glittered in the sunshine.

"I hope Elise's parents don't get trapped here," I said to nobody in particular.

"So do I!" Duncan was standing at the open door, looking out at the moors and the sea. "Her paps is the guest speaker at a big conference in less than a week."

"When are they supposed to go?" Malcolm asked. "I rather like having them here!"

"Not for a couple more days." Duncan had retrieved his phone from the charging point and was scrutinising it. "According to this," he told us, "the storm won't come this far north. It might just touch the southernmost part of Shetland – Sumburgh Head and Horse Island –"

"Nobody lives on Horse Island!" pointed out Malcolm.

"*Nei*," my son agreed, "but the storm might just touch it. Anyhow, I think Elise's parents will be okay."

We met up with them later that morning down on my beach. Harris had taken Malcolm's ponies and cart across the island to do some work at Holti's place, so it was just Elise and her parents from their bothy. Marigold had joined us, and Elise went with the two bairns, clambering over the rocks to the north of my little bay, hoping they might get a glimpse of the puffin colony which was established near to the top of the cliff just a little further round.

"So, are you happy with Elise's choices?" Malcolm asked. We knew them well enough by now to ask such a personal question.

"Aye." Elise's paps sounded very certain. "Young Harris is a little unusual but he's a good lad. Perhaps in earlier times we might have hoped for more for our lassie, but nowadays… This island seems like a much safer place to be than anywhere on the mainland. I fear for our future, but if anyone's going to survive all these catastrophes, it will be communities like yours."

"Don't be so depressing!" his wife admonished him. "People have realised now what we've done to our world! Governments are acting at last. We'll overcome the problems we're facing – you'll see!"

"My wife is an optimist!" Elise's paps commented. "I don't always share her sunny view of things… But I hope you're right, my love!"

"I agree with you about one thing," Malcolm was idly sorting through the pebbles where he was sitting. "En-Somi is a much safer place to live than some parts of the country!"

"Not quite as safe as I had imagined, though," Elise's mam said thoughtfully. "What about that container on the beach? Do you really have a drug problem? How on earth does anyone get hold of anything out here?"

"Perhaps they grow their own?" Elise's paps suggested.

"*Aja*," Malcolm agreed. "Where there's a will… But yesterday was the first indication I've had of any drug use on En-Somi. We ought to talk to Lyle…"

The bairns came clambering back over the rocks at that point.

"Duncan might know!" Malcolm commented. "Or Marigold." Then, speaking directly to the bairns as they settled on the rocks, "Do either of you know anything about *En-Som-in-Fedii* using drugs?"

"*Nei,*" Marigold sounded certain. "My paps, he says that there was a lot of drug use when he was growing up. It wasn't so unusual to see syringes on beaches in those days, and lots of people took stuff in the refugee camps. He absolutely hated it. But not here. Over at the old airport, people drank a lot, but there weren't any drugs..."

"A few people tried stuff out when we were over in Lerwick," Duncan told us. "Nothing heavy, you know?" Then he must have seen the horror on my face. "Not me, Mam! Nor Alana! We weren't in that crowd!"

★★★

Duncan and Marigold went on ahead while the rest of us stayed on the beach, swapping email addresses and vaguely discussing the possibility of Elise's parents retiring to En-Somi. We headed back to my bothy when our stomachs started to rumble.

"I hate the thought that she might do that," Marigold was saying, as we entered my bothy a few minutes later. The bairns were preparing a bread-and-cheese lunch, washing salad and arranging it in a wooden bowl, and setting it out on the counter for us to help ourselves. "We're talking about Elin," Marigold told me. "Duncan doesn't think she's use drugs, but I'm not so sure..."

"She might be a bit wild just now," Duncan chipped in. "But she's not a fool!"

"*Nei,* but if everyone else was…"

"Well, she came home the next morning, didn't she? And today she's posted about a new song she's started to write, called 'Hot, Hot Summer'. Look, she's posted a selfie, at home with her *langspil* on her lap. Does that look like a lassie who's gone off the rails?"

We peered over Duncan's shoulder to view the posting. I thought Elin looked tired, maybe a little pale, but otherwise quite normal.

"Perhaps it was just one night of rebellion?" I suggested. I was torn between thinking that all this concern was a fuss about nothing, and that same lurking sense of foreboding that I had first felt after talking to Olaf.

We were all quiet for a moment, thinking about the bairn.

Then, "*Nei*," Marigold told us. "She's been changing for a while. I don't know what's the matter with her…"

***

The *Oyrod* had become much more active since the balance of power had shifted. Well, that may be a little unfair, since it was the old, *harkrav*-dominated *Oyrod* that had introduced us to the internet and to wind turbines. By the time I'm telling you about now, and under the new administration, the council was having regular open meetings and holding them alternately in Storhaven and Gamla Hus, so the *bondii* were much more likely to attend.

The forecasters were wrong about the storm. It seemed to hover over the west of Europe for a couple of days and then come north to hit En-Somi the afternoon after Elise's parents left. They made it as far as Lerwick and had to weather the chaos there, but I think they were home in time for Elise's paps' big conference. Meanwhile we were quite busy preparing the meeting house to host a council meeting, which meant braving the driving rain to venture up to the village to put out chairs and mugs for dandelion tea. I think that was the first time we used wooden beakers instead of glass. Harris had made a full set and it was a relief, really, because they were unbreakable. We couldn't easily replace any glass that was broken by then, and we hadn't developed any pottery skills.

It must still have been early August. The bairns were not back at school yet and the evenings were still quite light, although we were all aware that the storm we had just experienced could be a foretaste of a hard winter.

We met in the evening, by which time the rain had stopped and everything seemed to be steaming. It was still light until 9.30 or 10 o'clock and there would be a full moon – walking home in the cooler night air would be a pleasure for many people when the decisions were made. Malcolm was the chairperson and introduced the business in a relaxed manner. There was a full complement of *oyrodii,* although some of the representatives complained about having to come over from Floirean's Cnoc. They seemed not to consider the distances people like the MacLoughlans had needed to travel when the meetings were regularly held in Storhaven.

I seem to remember that there were always some routine matters. The island finances were published online by then, and there were usually questions about some aspect of our expenditure. Once the new *Oyrod* had been elected, the punitive taxes imposed on those *bondii* with access to land had been reversed, but now islanders with higher incomes (and that meant the *harkrav*) tended to query quite ordinary outgoings. Was that the occasion when they debated, at length, the upgrading of the internet connection and computers in the Storhaven school? I think it might have been. Anyway, it was certainly that evening when the question of rising sea levels was first formally introduced. Don't misunderstand me, we had all been aware of the effect of all that melting ice, and individually we had taken what action we could. But that evening Mirren, one of our *nasyonii* or police officers, raised the question of protecting any low-lying land that was at risk.

"We can't fight nature," she told us. "But we can work with her. I know that the barley fields on the edge of Frigg Moor are safe – Mac and I were discussing it yesterday. But I wonder if anyone knows of any other areas we might need to protect? I'm still new here. Is there any common land beyond the summer harbour here in Hus that we ought to consider?"

Various *bondii* looked at each other and there was a low murmur. Mirren had raised a good point. One or two of the small number of *harkrav* who were there were heard to comment to each other, "More expenditure!"

Beyond these small, personal interchanges, nobody said anything for a minute or two. I suppose, like me, we were all considering the coastal areas near us. My beach had changed shape in the last few years when the waves washed away a grassy bank, but now the bare rock the sea had exposed looked like a fortress, I didn't think it likely I would see any more significant erosion.

It was Si who spoke up. "What about the land where the old airport is?" he wondered. "It's quite low. Should we be finking of doing anyfing there?"

There was a chorus of responses.

"Isn't it protected by sand dunes?"

"Has it ever flooded?"

"It's just wasteland!" (This from a *harkrav* woman. No *bondi* ever considered that land could be a waste!)

"Doesn't Jarvis still live out there?"

"You can grow stuff there," Si insisted. "When we was living in that ruin, we grew spuds. The surface of the runway's all breaking up. If we could some'ow get rid of it – you know, uncover the ground beneath – there'd be good land there. If we's thinking of trying to support ourselves, not depend on them ferries..."

There was another murmur, this time of general approval.

"It would cost a lot." This, of course, from another member of the *harkrav*.

"It would be a big job." Lyle was thinking of the practicalities. "And we don't have any heavy machinery on the island to break up the paved areas and demolish the old airport buildings."

"What about Jarvis?" Harry was concerned. "We can't just evict him!"

"Who owns that land, anyhow?"

"It could be a project for next year," suggested Robert. "Like when we rebuilt the track down to the summer harbour. When we all agreed to spend at least three working days on the job."

Malcolm hadn't said anything; he had just let people think it through. Now he stepped in. "We probably need to do some more research," he suggested. "We need to pin down who owns that land – I seem to remember that it might be some sort of trust. And we probably ought to get someone over from Shetland or Aberdeen to work out how best to get the land back into condition for agriculture."

There were nods of approval. Even the *harkrav* agreed with Malcolm, although I suspected it was just because we'd put off any actual action.

"In the meantime," Mirren hadn't quite finished, "should we at least do something to protect the land from high tides and storms? I've seen places where people have piled up rocks between the dunes and the sea – they can be quite effective."

Again, there was a general air of agreement, although I'm sure that I wasn't alone in thinking that Mirren's suggestion sounded like hard work.

"I'll see if I can persuade some of the young people in Storhaven to help," Mirren announced optimistically. "They're not all working on the land or fishing, the way the Hus bairns are."

"Good luck with that!" Robert was not impressed by the youth on the eastern side of En-Somi.

***

I remember that we were all thinking about self-sufficiency by then. I feared that Elise's mam had been over-optimistic: the hope that the governments of the world or the big commercial conglomerates might realise the urgency of the situation with our changed and changing climate was fading. As quickly as targets were set and resolutions made, those with the real power had found ways of getting round them. I suppose the opportunities for immediate profit were too tempting, compared with the hope of a better future. The world seemed more and more chaotic. Millions of people were on the move, hoping to get to this or that country which was thought to be safer, or escaping famine, drought, flooding, or the wars that broke out over scarce resources. We recognised how sheltered we were on En-Somi despite our bleak terrain and our isolation. In fact, our bleak terrain and our isolation were the very things that were protecting us.

It can only have been a few weeks later, about the time that the bairns went back to school, that the *Oyrod* met again; this time in the kirk in Storhaven. There were fewer people from Hus there, I remember, but Malcolm and I had taken the ponies and cart, with Alana, Marigold and my Duncan. Andy Kullander was supposed to make up their usual foursome, but right at the last minute he pulled out.

"He says he's too tired," Duncan told us, looking at his phone. "Again!"

We treated the bairns to a meal at The Castle before the meeting. They were growing up fast and were fun to have around – even if their conversation sometimes had a smattering of words I didn't recognise, gleaned from social media.

We were encouraged to tell a member of the *Oyrod* in advance if we wanted something additional to be discussed, although it wasn't a regulation. On the agenda that evening the one word 'orchard' appeared. Most people didn't know what the item referred to, but Malcolm and I had discussed it at home. I remember being gratified when Malcolm introduced the topic and asked Harry to speak. Harry had been a refugee and a slave, but since settling into his bothy with Mandy and her two bairns over beyond Yanni Sinclair's home, he had slotted quickly into the Gamla Hus community. He and Si often went out with Yanni to fish in the summer, and Harry and Mandy had established one of the largest and most successful vegetable patches west of Fyrtarn Fjell. A tall, grey-haired man, Harry rarely spoke but seemed always to listen intently. He was there that evening with Si – it turned out that the two men had walked over and were staying overnight with Tom, the ferryman.

Harry came up to the front to address us all. "I bin thinking," he told us, still speaking in his southern way. "We's done well this year, what wiv the good fishing and the spuds doing so well, but we's not been able to import much. I's concerned that we need to keep a varied diet – I suggests what we try growing apples."

There was a murmur among the assembled crowd.

"We're too far north," instructed one person.

"The wrong sort of soil!" said another.

"Too great a risk of frost when the trees are flowering," volunteered one of the remaining *harkrav* representatives.

"*Nei*," Harry mildly corrected everyone. He was standing in front of the wooden table from which communion was served, and somehow his location seemed to give him authority. "I's bin doing some research. There's a sort of apple what was developed in Scotland. It's called a James Grieve. It 'as frost-'ardy flowers and it fruits in September, before the worst of the storms..."

"The storms are totally unpredictable nowadays!" called out one of the Storhaven *bondii*.

Harry was patient. "*Aja*," he agreed. "But in a way, that's my point. I likes to 'ave fruit to eat, and there ain't no way we's going to be able to import it! We needs to be self-sufficient!"

"Have you ever grown apples?" It was a genuine question from Sigrid, not an objection.

"*Nei*, but I thinks I could," the tall man responded. He wasn't being proud, he was stating a fact.

Yanni stood. "I think he could too," he told us. "He's got green fingers! Anyhow, isn't it worth a try? I'd love to have fresh fruit now and again!"

There were general sounds of agreement from around the kirk.

"What would you need, to make a start?" Malcolm asked.

Harry smiled. "Well... we needs a west-facing orchard, so as no frost thaws too quickly in the mornings," he told us. "That's what does for the blossoms. And the land needs to be well drained. Me and Yanni, we fought what the side of the 'ill facing over towards Marie and Malcolm – that might be a grand place."

"Over beyond Hus," explained Si, for the sake of any folk on the east of En-Somi who didn't know where Yanni farmed.

"South-west facing," explained Yanni.

"We needs to build a wall to shelter the trees," Harry continued, "and I dare say as we could use some 'elp with that, although I can dig the drainage. I knows about that. Then we needs to buy the trees and plant 'em. We 'as to plant 'em when they's dormant, so it would be good to try for this autumn; maybe November?"

One of the *harkrav* representatives rose then, and Malcolm stood aside. "It sounds like an expensive and probably a futile experiment to me. Nobody grows apples this far north!"

"*Nei!*" Harry had done his research. "There's people – First Nation people in Canada – what 'ave grown apples inside the Arctic Circle! In a place called Inuvik! If they does it, we can too!"

Verity stood then; wee Joel on her hip with his thumb in his mouth. "I have to say," she told us, "I think Harry's right. And not just because I like apples! We can't depend on imports even now and the climate's only going to get worse..."

Again, there were grunts of agreement.

"Well then, let's vote on it, shall we?" Malcolm asked.

The decision was very clear-cut. Only two people didn't raise their hand and, of those, I think one might have been asleep!

★★★

It was on the way home that we had a surprising encounter. By common consent, bairns of thirteen or over were allowed to vote at meetings of the *Oyrod*, and as a general rule the teenagers sat together at the back of the room, away from their parents. Duncan was regaling us with an amusing mistake on Christian's part. Marigold had been talking about tectonic plates and Christian had called them 'Teutonic plates'. He had been sure that two of them must meet in Germany, because didn't 'Teutonic' refer to the ancient Germanic people? It seemed that poor Christian had laboured under this delusion since primary school!

It was dark by the time we arrived back in Hus and dropped Alana and Marigold off at their homes. The three of us who remained had just reached the place where the path to my bothy deviates from the track to Malcolm's, although, as usual, we were all going back to my place, when Duncan suddenly said, "Is that someone sitting on the wall?"

We all peered ahead in the gloom. The figure moved and came towards us. Of course, it was Jarvis, our resident hermit, who wandered the island alone and might turn up anywhere.

"*Hei*, pal!" Malcolm greeted him. "How's things?"

"Things is good," Jarvis told us. "'Ello Marie. Is that Duncan? 'Ello, kid!"

"We've just been to a meeting in Storhaven," I told the man. "And now we're going home for a mug of hot chocolate. Do you fancy some?"

Jarvis seemed to hesitate slightly, then he agreed. "I likes 'ot chocolate," he told us. "Wiv a biscuit or two to dunk in it!"

We climbed down from the cart as we reached the place where, in those days, we still kept it, and Duncan and I took the harnesses off the ponies. The track to my bothy grew narrow at that point. Later, of course, we widened the path and built proper stabling for the ponies and a shed for the cart, between my home and the wind turbine. Jarvis led the way after that. I think that by then he must have known every inch of the island – better even than people who had lived all their lives on En-Somi.

Jarvis had only been to my home once before as far as I can remember, and on that occasion, we had all sat on the slate area in front, looking out at the sea. Malcolm took the ponies to their temporary stable and our visitor stood aside to let us enter the bothy, then waited at the door for Malcolm to come back. I thought that the man was shy, so I didn't make any comments; just filled the kettle and opened the tin of chocolate powder. Then Malcolm returned. Jarvis had obviously noticed that we all took off our shoes on the way in. As always, he was bare-foot, and I thought he looked a little embarrassed as he glanced down at his dirty feet.

"I better stay out 'ere," he suggested. "I's a bit grubby."

"Nonsense!" Malcolm held the door wide open, encouraging the man to enter. "Come and take a seat!" He indicated the rocking chairs, and then stepped across to the kitchen area to take over from me. "Does everyone want a drink?" he asked. "Marie, have we got any of those biscuits left, the ones the bairns made?"

Soon, we were all seated, sipping our drinks and making the most of Duncan and Marigold's cookery expertise. I noticed that Jarvis looked a little uncomfortable. He kept shifting in his chair and moving his feet around on the floor.

Finally, I asked, "Are you okay, Jarvis?"

"Oh, yeah! Yeah!" He looked at me and smiled. "I's just surprised what your floor is 'ot. Well, not 'ot, but warm. I never knowed a floor like this before."

"It's underfloor heating," Duncan explained. "It comes on automatically if the temperature drops below eighteen. It shows that the weather is changing – the heating hasn't come on for weeks!"

Jarvis looked from one to another of us. "Well, I be blowed!" he remarked, and returned to dunking his third biscuit.

We talked a little about this and that – the storm that had just passed, Yanni's new hut for drying fish, and the puffin colony, which it turned out Jarvis had been keeping an eye on.

"Them vicious gulls!" he told us. "They'd take the babies given 'alf a chance, and them puffins, they only 'as one puffling a year, as far as I can tell. So I bin sitting on top of the cliff protecting 'em."

"Oh wow!" Duncan was really impressed. "I wish we'd thought of that!"

"Weren't no need!" Jarvis reassured my son. "I bin sleeping up there sometimes. When it were so 'ot. You kids 'ave lives to lead; fings to do." Then he started to look more serious. "As a matter of fact, that's what I come to talk to you about," he told us.

"Puffins?" Duncan was obviously surprised.

"Go ahead!" Malcolm, who was seated on my settle, leaned forward a little, ignoring Duncan.

"I been watching them kids," Jarvis told us. "Not you, Duncan, though I always keeps an eye on Marigold, so as nobody 'arms 'er. But I seen them yobs over in the town, and then I sees this little girl – looks no older than a kid – and she bin wiv 'em, and I doesn't fink what it's right!"

"What girl?" asked Duncan. "What does she look like?"

That wasn't actually a very helpful question for Jarvis. We had discovered several years earlier that for some reason Jarvis had real difficulty telling people apart. He seemed to depend on clues that the rest of us wouldn't need, like where he saw someone or what they were wearing.

"She's just a little thing," Jarvis said. "I mean, I suppose what she's a teenager now, maybe a bit younger'n Marigold? But skinny. Always seems to wear black. 'As a lovely singing voice.

When we was first free and she were just a small kid, she used to go to that 'arbour what you only use in the summer. She would be on 'er own, and sit on that rock where I seen you all make a fire once. And she used to sing – always sad songs. I fought what she were like a mermaid." Jarvis paused for a moment. "I don't see 'er there no more. I didn't scare 'er off or nofing; I never let 'er know I was there. But I suppose she's growed up a bit now…"

"Elin!" exclaimed Duncan under his breath. "It has to be Elin!"

"*Aja*," Malcolm and I agreed in unison.

"Well, I's worried about 'er," Jarvis told us. "Them yobs, they ain't no good, and there don't seem to be nobody looking out for 'er. So, I fought maybe you, Marie – and Malcolm too…"

"You'd like us to keep an eye on her?" Malcolm asked.

"Well…" Jarvis looked uncomfortable. "I don't want no one messing 'er up. Not them yobs, but not no do-gooders, neither! I don't want nobody to fink they knows better than that kid, not even you, 'cause you knows, that's what they fought about me when I were a youngster. And they didn't know what were good for me at all!"

"We're worried about her too," I reassured the man. "And we're really grateful to you for coming to us. We don't really know Elin, though. I'm not sure where we'd start."

"She hasn't got a mam, you see," Duncan explained to Jarvis. "Her paps has all the work to do around their bothy, and he goes out fishing. I suppose she's on her own a lot when there's no school."

Malcolm was looking thoughtful. "*Aja*," he agreed. "And even when there *is* school… the bairn is learning online now, isn't she? It's a pretty isolated life. Does she have any friends her own age to study with, the way you four get together?"

"There's really only Christian," Duncan told us. "He's a year or more older than Elin. There isn't anyone exactly her age on this side of the island…"

"So, I suppose she has a rather lonely time of it..." I was thinking aloud.

"I doesn't know what's right to do," Jarvis told us, a worried frown on his face. "Ain't no good interfering in 'er life. I seen it when I were a young 'un. Them teachers or youf workers, they tells kids what to do and what not to do, but they ain't got no idea why them kids is behaving the way they does. Then them kids, they go off and do the opposite. And then there's trouble."

"*Aja*, that's just the way it goes a lot of the time," agreed Malcolm, who had dealt with more than his fair share of troubled youth during his working life. "We'll give the situation some thought." Then, seeing how troubled Jarvis still looked, he added, "We won't try to take over her life, the way you felt those teachers and youth workers did. We'll just look out for her."

But what on earth can we do? I wondered.

CHAPTER 5

One of Jamie MacLoughlan's sheep had somehow fallen into a marshy pit between two huge, grey rocks on Michaelmas Fjell. Jamie texted us soon after breakfast the following day.

Duncan was still in his pyjamas, eating porridge and sending messages to his friends. "Can Alana come here for our Norwegian lesson?" he asked. "And then Marigold for advanced maths?"

"Of course," I answered. "But Malcolm and I need to go and help Jamie. There's tea and biscuits but no coffee – we've run out."

"Tea's better anyhow," my son told me. "It boosts your immune system. Coffee just makes you stressed."

"I quite like a mug or two of stress-inducing caffeine in the mornings," Malcolm commented, putting on his boots. "It helps me to wake up. But tea is good too... are you ready, Marie? I think we could go up over the top of the moor, don't you?"

"Be careful!" warned my son. "It'll be muddy!"

In fact, it wasn't too bad. We met Jamie, standing and looking down at the trapped sheep, the wind blowing his hair around his head.

"The daft beastie!" he commented cheerfully. "One of last year's lambs. You'd think she'd know better by now!"

"She's lucky she slipped here," Malcolm commented. "There're places where we could never have reached her, just a little further on."

"Oh, *aja*," Jamie agreed. "I nearly fell to my death once when I was a laddie, trying to rescue some *amdatchi* yearling! My paps had told me not to risk my neck doing anything he wouldn't do, but I was determined to prove to him how capable I was! But we should be able to save this one without risking our necks!"

He climbed down between the rocks until he was a little lower than the trapped sheep, and balanced with his feet either side of the narrowing crevice, green with lichen and slick with moisture. "Ready!" he called up to us. "Make sure your footing's secure – we don't want either of you falling down this hole!"

Then Jamie heaved from below while Malcolm and I tugged from above, holding onto the poor, scared animal wherever we could. She objected with a few plaintive baas and we slithered around a bit on the mossy, muddy surface, but at last we managed to heave the stupid creature back onto safe ground.

"Don't let her fall back in!" warned Jamie, peering over the top of the rocks.

So we pushed her by the rump over towards a flatter part of the peaty moorland. The daft animal didn't seem to know or acknowledge the difficulty she had been in. She just wriggled and scampered away, stopping near a rocky outcrop to graze on the grass growing there.

Jamie clambered up and wiped his muddy hands on his trousers. He was grinning. "Well, there's one good thing about sheep," he commented, retrieving his backpack, which had been left a few feet away. "They're never going to have nervous breakdowns!" He glanced across at the munching animal. "She's already forgotten about her adventures!"

We stood together, the three of us, drinking tea from Jamie's flask, passing the cup round. Jamie flicked a piece of moss from his trousers, his brow slightly furrowed.

"I saw Jarvis this morning," he told us, staring across at Fyrtarn Fjell. "I was up early – our cockerel woke me and the morning seemed too good to waste."

"He's been sleeping on top of the cliffs," Malcolm told our neighbour. "Protecting the puffin chicks from predatory gulls. Our Duncan thinks he's quite a hero."

"Hmm…" Jamie took the cup I was passing to him. "But…" He hesitated, then went on. "First I saw Jarvis along by my south field – the place where the old folks used to cut the peat." *Well, nothing surprising about that,* I thought. "But then I saw wee Elin – well, it must have been her, although she was wearing one of those green waxed jackets, much too big for her. Heading for the *fjell* by the look of it. Coming home, I would have said."

"Ah!" Malcolm acknowledged Jamie's concern.

"Why was the bairn out so early?" Jamie sounded unsure of himself. "And I thought… it looked to me as if… well, I wondered if Jarvis was following Elin. If it *was* Elin. Well, it must have been her… A wee lass like that alone on the moors! Do you think Jarvis would hurt her? You know him, after all. I don't."

"*Nei.*" I would have trusted Jarvis even before he had spoken to us about the bairn. "He won't hurt Elin. He's probably just checking she's all right. He does that, you know. He keeps an eye on Marigold too."

Jamie looked from one to the other of us. "Well…" he said, still sounding hesitant. "If you're sure…"

"Marie's right," Malcolm responded. "He's worried about Elin. He won't hurt her."

Suddenly, Jamie grinned. "Like the song says," he almost chuckled. "*Dark and lonely, foreign stranger, saving us from hidden danger.* That's what Olaf's song says, isn't it?" Then he looked serious again. "Let's hope that's the way it really is!"

★★★

When we arrived back at the bothy, all four bairns were sitting around in the living area, laptops at the ready and notebooks and textbooks scattered around on the floor. Andy, who was revising for his Highers, and Alana who must have been following a lesson of her own, were both wearing headphones. Marigold and Duncan were sitting on the floor by the fire, talking.

"*Hei*, Marie!" Marigold said. "Duncan's Norwegian teacher says I speak the language as well as he does!"

"She arrived here at the end of our lesson," my son explained, "so we introduced her. Marigold is taught by Stephani."

"Well done, Marigold!" exclaimed Malcolm, who had come in after me. "I never did really master any other languages."

"But more importantly," Duncan continued, "we've been talking about Elin."

"Ah!" I sat on the only available rocking chair, prepared to hear what they had to say.

"We think you were right last night, when you said that Elin must be lonely," Marigold started. "And not only that, but she's spent all her time with men – with her paps and Olaf. And they're both really kind, but…"

"So, we thought we'd ask her to join our study group," Duncan continued.

Alana and Andy, aware that we were talking, had taken off their headphones to listen.

"Maybe she won't want to go off with boys like the ones who came to our end-of-term meal," Alana added, "if she feels she's got a group of friends over here."

I glanced at Malcolm. He was standing at the foot of the ladder up to our sleeping platform, about to take up a fresh pile of laundry. He winked at me and smiled.

"That's a brilliant idea!" I told the assembled bairns. "And very kind!"

★★★

There was something wrong with Olaf. He was an old man, of course – I didn't know how old, but Malcolm told me that

Olaf's hair had been white even when Malcolm was at school. "He lived over here by then, in that little bothy on the edge of the village," my partner told me. "We didn't see as much of him on the east of the island. But he came several times to the school to teach us some of the traditional ballads. We all knew who he was."

The bairns were back in school and the evenings were getting shorter, but the weather had warmed up again after yet another storm. Petter had put the tables out on the track in front of the *fi'ilsted* again as he had done earlier in the summer, and resurrected the old fish-oil lamps they used to use before we had electricity on the island. He stood a lamp on each table, giving the scene an almost magical air. The midge season was over and most crofters stopped working when the light faded around eight thirty, so a fair smattering of villagers were to be seen drinking tea or something stronger as the long, summer dusk descended. Malcolm and I took to walking up to the village after we had eaten, and spending an hour or so with whoever happened to be there.

Olaf wasn't much of a drinker. I had seen him take a dram or two, but mostly he was a dandelion tea man. We joined him one evening as he sat there, a huge jug in front of him, with ice floating on top and melting gently.

"So, my friends," he greeted us. "How are things in the *Bjornhuss*?" He meant my bothy, of course, which in theory still belonged to my ex.

"Good," I told him. "Oh, thanks – just tea for me!"

"Have you got any of Jamie's whisky still?" Malcolm wondered, speaking to Petter who was hovering at our table. "A wee glass would go down well…"

"Our salad recovered from the storm," I told the old man. "We've got a bumper crop of tomatoes – it's the first time I've grown them. Would you like any? And Harris is making us a new barrel to store more fish."

"Skilled work, that!" Olaf was approving. "It's not everyone who can make barrels! That laddie is turning out better than his parents dared hope!"

"*Aja*," Malcolm agreed. "They're the ideal neighbours. Elise has brought my kale beds back to life. I don't think *Mori-mori* Cadha (he meant the previous owner of his bothy) had been up to gardening for several years."

"*Nei*," Olaf agreed. "There's little pleasure in growing old. It will have grieved her to see her garden going to weeds..." There was a note of sadness in Olaf's voice. It made me look at him afresh. He had always seemed so positive about life – serene, even. Now he just sounded like any old man regretting his youth.

Malcolm looked concerned. "But *Mori-mori* Cadha could look back on a life well spent," he pointed out. "And when she died, there were many who mourned her. Perhaps none of us can ask for more than that!"

"I wouldn't ask for more," agreed Olaf, but he sounded sad.

"Olaf," I said, trying to comfort him, "you'll leave a legacy greater than most! Think of all the songs you've written; the history we *En-Som-in-Fedii* will never forget, thanks to you!"

"I fear they may forget..." Olaf was swirling the melting ice round and round in his glass. "Not you; not your generation. Maybe not your bairns. But after that... I think there'll be nobody left to teach them the songs. And it will be my fault. I put all my eggs in one basket..."

We realised he was thinking of Elin.

"I wouldn't despair." Malcolm tried to encourage the old man. "That wee lassie is young yet..."

"*Aja*," agreed Olaf with a sigh. "So she is! So she is!" But he didn't sound convinced. Then he reached around to where his stick was lying on the ground. "Well, it's bedtime for me! I wish you a good night's rest and blessings in the morning!"

And with that he left.

★★★

"Mam," Duncan asked me when he emerged from his bed the following morning, "have you heard Elin's new song?"

"*Nei*," I answered. "Is it good?"

"It depends what you think of as good!" Duncan remarked disapprovingly. "Listen to this!"

He passed his phone to me. He was showing me a piece of video: Elin singing and accompanying herself on that beautiful *langspil* given to her by Olaf only a few months earlier. It was a stunning piece of music, I realised at once. Between each short verse Elin played a complicated and haunting instrumental that seemed to have echoes of waves breaking and wind blowing. Her voice was achingly sad, but the words were – well, the word that came to my mind was 'tragic'.

Probably you have heard this song if you listen to that kind of music at all, but I'll tell you the words in case you've never listened to 'Hot, Hot Summer'. I can still hear Elin singing them as I recite them now – her harrowing young voice, that little catch in her throat as she sang the last line. And I can see her, too, as clearly as when Duncan first showed me her performance. She had long, mousy-blonde hair and her face was still childlike. I remember that she was wearing make-up: a lot of dark shades that made her look alien; not like an islander at all. And the words – were they prophetic?

We're lying on the beach, you and me,
The sand is cool, the sea is calm,
The joy is coursing through my veins,
And I am free

We're lying in your bed, you and me.
The sheets are tangled, the light is low.
Your touch is on my body,
And I am free

We're sitting on the cliffs, you and me.
There are stars in the sky and shrooms in my blood,
And air all around –
And I am free

We are lying in our graves, you and me.
The peat is over us, rocks below.
Short lives but full,
Forever free

"Wow!" I exclaimed. "It's amazing – and terrible!"

"*Aja*, that's what I thought." Duncan sounded serious. "And look how many 'likes' it's got, and she only posted it last night. In fact, at three this morning!"

Malcolm came in from checking the ponies. "What are you so interested in?" he wanted to know.

Duncan passed him the phone. "Look!" he commanded.

Malcolm started to watch the video. He played it through twice, then clicked the site off and passed the phone back to Duncan. "Well," he said, "she's gifted, that's for sure!"

We stood and looked at each other, all stunned, I suppose.

Then, "It might all be in her imagination, you know," Malcolm reminded us. "She's still a bairn. What is she, thirteen? She could be basing the whole song on things she's seen on TV. We shouldn't jump to conclusions."

"I suppose 'shrooms' are magic mushrooms?" I asked. "Like the ones you found in that container on the beach? Do they grow on En-Somi?"

"They might," Duncan told me. "I don't know; I haven't heard of them being used here. But you know, over in Storhaven…" He paused. "That first verse – you know, *lying on the sand* – Elin did go down to the beach with that group of lads. It might be real – I mean, it might be based on the life she's living now…"

"Wouldn't her paps know?" I asked feebly. "Wouldn't he stop her?"

Malcolm was frowning. "It isn't easy, raising bairns on your own," he told us. "Elin's paps has spent nights out fishing; he teams up with Yanni and his crew. How would he know what Elin did while he was away?"

"I'll ask her to join our study group. I'll ask her today!" Duncan said. "We meant to invite her sooner but she hasn't been at the meeting house."

Malcolm rested his hand lightly on my son's shoulder. "Well done, lad!" he said quietly, and Duncan turned and smiled at him. They were good together, those two.

CHAPTER 6

Mirren, the *nasyoni* from Storhaven, came over to see Lyle. The two were in regular contact via phone and text, but they had their own areas to care for, and for a while there had been no serious problems on the island. Lyle thought that Mirren had a more difficult job than he did. She had a bigger mix of people on her patch, and some of the *harkrav* seemed to labour under the impression that when the authorities talked about the police serving the people, they meant that Mirren was actually their servant. She had needed to be very firm when she first arrived about the tasks that were in her job description and those that were not. She came over, we heard later, to warn Lyle that she had heard rumours of a drug problem over in Storhaven.

"Of course, there might be nothing to it. The song that's doing the rounds – 'Hot, Hot Summer'– might have given people the idea," she told Lyle. "But I fear there could be some truth to it. I worry about the youth up on Floirean's Cnoc. They were in school on the mainland and who knows what habits they might have picked up there. Although some of our own bairns are not beyond reproach, of course…"

Mirren, on the other hand, suspected that Lyle's work was harder. He was responsible for the majority of outlying bothies on the island, and the people in and around Gamla Hus were very self-sufficient, and therefore less likely to ask for Lyle's intervention until matters had become serious. That was probably why Elin's paps hadn't mentioned his concerns about Elin.

In the event, it was Malcolm and me who told Lyle about the magic mushrooms on the beach. We should have told him sooner, of course, although I don't think it would have made any difference to the way things turned out.

It was probably a day or two after Elin had posted 'Hot, Hot Summer'. It was a Sunday. Usually a few of us gathered in the meeting house for a time of worship. To begin with, it had just been Verity, Malcolm and me. Verity had been ordained in the Presbyterian Church but had left; Malcolm and I were beginning to experiment with meditation and prayer. Perhaps you could say we were all seekers, although we were consciously looking to the Quakers for a way forward. Initially, Lyle didn't attend these mostly silent meetings. That had changed when wee Bonnie, their second child, had chosen to arrive in the middle of a hurricane, meaning that Verity had been forced to manage with only Sigrid and Rose in attendance. The following morning, Verity, of course, hadn't come to the meeting house, but Lyle had. About halfway through our hour of worship, he had stood, taken the Bible from the table in the middle, and read from it:

For thou hast been a strength to the poor, a strength to the needy in his distress, a refuge from the storm, a shadow from the heat, when the blast of the terrible ones is as a storm against the wall.

Then he had put the Bible back on the table, and said, "In the middle of last night, when her labour was really hard, my Verity said these words. They seemed so fitting. She needed strength and we could hear the blast of the storm against our walls. I didn't know what she was reciting, but this morning she told me. I'm not much of a one for the Bible myself... But anyhow, I've come to give thanks to whoever or whatever is the refuge from storms and the giver of strength." Then, he had grinned. "I don't know who 'the terrible ones' are, though!"

We had all sat in silence again. Unlike the kirk in Storhaven, our meeting house is not at all soundproof, and I remember that we could hear the gusting wind around the rebuilt chimneys which were no longer used.

After a while, Malcolm had risen to his feet. "I think I know who the terrible ones are," he had told us. "Or, at least, what. I don't think they're people at all. I think the terrible ones are those thoughts and fears that seem to attack us; that make us weak. When I was working, 'the terrible ones' were the voices in the heads of the street lads which told them that they would never amount to anything. When we felt so threatened and desperate about the high taxes a few years ago, 'the terrible ones' were our suspicions that we wouldn't survive; even that we would have to leave En-Somi." He had been quiet for a moment and a gull perched on the roof had given a loud squawk as if in agreement. Then Malcolm had looked directly at Lyle. "I was at the birth of two of my bairns," he had said. "It made me grateful, if I'm honest, that I'm a man. I saw with my own eyes that there came a time, especially with wee Beth, when my wife felt she just couldn't go on. I wonder if that urge to give up wasn't a 'blast of the terrible ones'?"

We had all been silent again. From the track outside the meeting house, quite loudly, we had heard a bairn's voice: "Goal!" There had been a ripple of laughter among our small, reflective group.

Afterwards, we had all agreed that there had been something special about that meeting – I would say profound – and after that, although he was not there every week, Lyle had become a pretty regular attender.

He was there the Sunday following the release of Elin's song. All the bairns were discussing it, and there was much speculation about how much of it might reflect Elin's actual life, and how much it was just a song. Lyle and Harry were talking about it over beakers of tea that morning.

"Whether or not she's actually done those things," Harry was saying gravely, "it seems to show an unhealthy interest in stuff a wee girl ought not to be thinking about. I'd be worried if Mandy's lassie wrote a song like that!"

"*Aja*," Lyle agreed. "It *is* worrying, but I dare say it's all just in her imagination. We have no reason to think there are drugs on this side of the island and I doubt if the bairn ever goes to Storhaven – and definitely not to Floirean's Cnoc!"

"She wouldn't need to," Malcolm interrupted. "Go over to Storhaven, I mean. Don't you remember that those lads came here? And Elin went with them to the beach? And then we found some magic mushrooms down there…"

Lyle put down his beaker and gave Malcolm a steady look. "I wouldn't have minded knowing about that earlier," he said, mildly reprimanding us.

Malcolm looked embarrassed. "*Aja*, I'm sorry, but it was just a couple of days before the storm and you were over in Fremdes Haven… But yes, we should have told you. I'm sorry."

"Have those lads been over here, to the west of the island, since then?" I guessed Harry was thinking about his adopted bairns.

"I haven't heard from Duncan that they have," I told him. "And I'm sure he'd tell us. Don't you think so, Malcolm?" *But according to Jamie*, I was thinking, *Elin has been over to Storhaven since – and maybe even to Floirean's Cnoc.*

★★★

My son was as good as his word. When I arrived back from my knitting cooperative a few days later, he was serving tea to Marigold, Alana and Elin.

I glanced around my one room. "No Andy?" I asked.

"He isn't feeling well," Marigold told me. "He came down to the meeting house right after morning classes but then went home almost at once. He looked awful."

"Poor Andy! But *hei*, Elin. Welcome!"

"Thanks." She was sitting on one of the rocking chairs, rocking gently, and for some reason it reminded me of those deprived children you see on documentaries, imprisoned in cots in orphanages in Eastern Bloc countries because there are too few nurses to care for them properly. She was wearing that heavy, dark make-up round her eyes, and she looked drawn.

"What have you been studying today?" I asked, trying to sound cheerful and normal. "Anything of interest?"

"Elin's got to write a review of *Sense and Sensibility*," Marigold told me. "I had to read it the year before last. I loved it – all those old-fashioned women and polite men! But you're not enjoying it, are you, Elin?"

"*Nei*," the bairn answered in a sulky voice. "I think it's silly! They think they're in love when they haven't even kissed each other yet, and an honourable man is supposed to marry a girl even if he's changed his mind and fallen in love with someone else! I mean, who would live a life like that? And how can I write a review? If I say what I really think, I'll get a D!"

Alana looked a little uncomfortable. "I didn't find it that easy to read," she admitted. "I think it was written for adults and now it's in the curriculum for thirteen-year-olds, but I liked it once I got into it. And doesn't it have a happy ending? Don't both girls end up marrying men they love?"

Elin looked exasperated. "Honestly, Alana, you sound just like the women in the book! There's more to life than getting married and living happily ever after!"

That was too much for Alana. "And how would you know?" she demanded. "My mam and paps married for love, and they're still happy! And I hope I will too, one day. Mam says that marrying Paps was the best thing she ever did."

Elin jumped to her feet, her face red. "Oh, you lot think you know so much, don't you? Here you are, studying away, being good, toeing the line, and for what? You don't even know you're alive! And don't you realise, by the time you've passed all those important exams and qualified from your wonderful universities, this life will be almost over? The climate is *wrecked*, the world is dying – we've killed it! You have to live your life *now*; you have to make the most of it!"

And with that, she grabbed her backpack and stormed out.

"Mm," commented Duncan. "Well, that idea didn't work out so well!"

CHAPTER 7

Andy continued to be unwell. A couple of days later, I walked up to the Kullander's place to see how he was. Fiona was in her kitchen when I arrived and we sat together over coffee (they hadn't run out yet), talking about our bairns.

"They never really got to the bottom of it, those specialists," Fiona told me. "They think it's something genetic – Alf's *paripari* seems to have had very similar symptoms as a lad. But by all accounts, he grew out of it. I hate to see Andy like this…"

I could imagine. "What do they recommend, those specialists?" I wondered.

Fiona chuckled. "Can't you guess? Fresh air, exercise, good food, not too much stress! But right now, all he wants to do is sleep. So that's what he's doing. The new doctor is coming over to look at him, any time now. She says she's no expert on these new, enfeebling sicknesses – that's what she called them. But she'll help if she can."

I was thinking about that word 'enfeebling'. It absolutely summed up Andy's condition as I had witnessed it. I reflected that the only time I had ever seen my Duncan sleeping in the daytime, once he was past the toddler stage, was when he'd been up all night. Of course, I didn't say so. "The others miss him," I told my friend.

"*Aja.*" Fiona smiled. "Did they tell you? They came up here yesterday. They wanted to know how Andy was, and they brought him some blaeberries that they'd picked on the moors. They're supposed to be a superfood, you know."

"*Nei*, they didn't mention it!" I was smiling too. "Did they tell you about their attempt to include Elin in their group?"

Fiona shook her head. "That was a good idea, although – did it work?"

"*Nei*," I told her sadly. "They ended up arguing over a book review and Elin stormed out."

"That poor wee lass!" responded Fiona.

★★★

Fiona's mention of blaeberries had given me an idea. I had seen some growing on the steep moorland between the Kullander's place and the track up to Fyrtarn Fjell a few weeks earlier. They might be nearly over by now, but if I could find enough, I could make a pie for pudding. It was not easy-going, although I was very sure-footed in those days. Still, the ground was relatively dry and the air was sweet with the smell of moorland plants. Although the midges had gone, there were bees everywhere, making the most of the lemon-scented ferns and the tiny violets that were still blooming among the rocks. From the village below, I could hear the voices of bairns playing, and from everywhere came the baaing of sheep and the cries of gulls. I felt, I remember, suddenly light-hearted.

Then I saw Elin. She was sitting on a rock with her back to me and she didn't turn although she must have heard my approach.

"Elin?" I said.

"Go away!" replied the bairn.

A part of me thought I should do just that. Teenagers need their space and ours is a small community. Perhaps all the speculation over 'Hot, Hot Summer' had got to her? Maybe her *paps* or Olaf had given her a hard time? But then I thought, *She's just a bairn with no mam and hadn't Jarvis asked us to look out for her*? "Are things a bit tough for you just now?" I asked to her hunched back.

"You could say that," muttered Elin.

I sat precariously on a rather squishy mound of turf behind the child. "They'll just be concerned for you," I suggested, guessing that it was the adults in Elin's life who had caused her to climb the moor on her own.

"Maybe," she answered, still not turning. She didn't sound convinced.

I wasn't sure what to say. I didn't have the experience that Malcolm had gained from all his years of social work, and my own son, I had come to realise, was unusually uncomplicated.

I suppose that staying quiet had been the right tactic. Elin turned on her rock and looked at me. "Were you ever friends with my mam?" she asked.

"*Nei*," I told her. "I was young when I first came to En-Somi and I didn't know anyone except Bjorn. It took me a while to get to know people..."

"She was pretty, my mam," the bairn continued. "But a wee bit unbalanced. That's what I've heard. Not *very* unbalanced, just a wee bit!"

"Who told you that?" I wondered.

"Nobody *told* me!" she exclaimed. "I overheard it. I thought it meant that she fell over easily. For years I thought that she died falling off a cliff. Because she was a wee bit unbalanced, you see."

"I thought it was cancer?" I asked.

"*Aja*, so it was!" agreed the bairn. "But that doesn't mean that she wasn't unbalanced too! They mean crazy, don't they? Doolally? Not quite right in the head?"

"I've never heard that," I told Elin honestly.

"You've probably never been told that she wasn't supposed to have any bairns, either?" The lassie sounded bitter. "I heard some men talking outside the *fi'ilsted* when I was just a wee thing, walking to school on my own for the first time. They said my paps was lucky that I seemed normal; that he and Mam had taken a risk having me. They were talking in dialect. I suppose they didn't realise how much I could hear – or understand."

I was quiet for a few minutes. Had people really said that, within earshot of a wee lassie who could so easily be damaged by thoughtless words? And was there any truth in it? "It just sounds like gossip to me," I commented. "I remember when your mam died, but I don't recall anyone telling me anything about your parents being advised not to have children. I was still with Bjorn then and I remember him saying he was glad your paps had you, because you would always remind him of the woman he loved. I know people were sad, but I don't think anyone was critical of your mam and paps. Not to me, anyhow."

"*Nei*, but then people tell you nice things, don't they?" Suddenly the bairn sounded angry. "You have a *nice* man and a *nice* bothy and a *nice* son who has *nice* friends... Everything in your world is wholesome and good. My world isn't like that."

I felt, I suppose, shocked. That Malcolm would have come across such disillusioned – even depressed – bairns in inner-city Edinburgh was one thing. It just hadn't ever occurred to me that any of our young people might suffer from such deep-seated unhappiness on En-Somi. "Oh, Elin!" I exclaimed feebly. "I'm so sorry you feel like that!"

Then, to my surprise, the bairn made a sort of lurch towards me and clung to me, sobbing into my shoulder. It was awkward – I mean, physically difficult. I wasn't very secure on my patch of hillside; it took all my strength and willpower to hold her and not to slip. But hold her I did, as her sobs slowly subsided. She felt so slight in my arms, so slim and light. A mere child. At last, she pulled away.

"I nearly knocked you over," she said and almost smiled. Her black eye make-up had streaked down her cheeks and over my jacket. She wiped her face with her hands. "Sorry!" she said. "Sorry! Sorry! Sorry! I shouldn't have done that! I was just... I won't... Anyhow, I'll be off now!" She jumped to her feet and started to clamber down the slope.

"Wait, Elin!" I called, but the bairn just gave a little wave with her hand. "Elin!" I called again. "Elin…" Then, realising that she wasn't going to stop, "Elin! You know where I am if you ever need me!"

But the bairn had gone. *Aja*, I thought to myself. *So, there it is again – another blast of the terrible ones.*

★★★

I had hoped to talk to Malcolm about my encounter with wee Elin as soon as I arrived home, but I walked into the bothy to find Duncan and Malcolm perched on the settle, Duncan in tears and Malcolm looking grave, with one hand resting gently on the arm of my son. Malcolm raised an eyebrow, in a way that I knew immediately meant, *There's trouble!*

"*Hei*," I greeted them, as I took off my shoes and hung up my jacket. "You both look as if you need a cup of tea."

Duncan looked up and gave me a watery grin. "Oh, Mam!" he told me. "You always know just the right thing to say or do!" Then he looked sideways, a little guiltily, at Malcolm. "And you do, too!" he reassured my partner.

"So, what's up?" I asked, as I filled the kettle and sat it back on its base.

For a moment, neither of them spoke. Perhaps each was waiting for the other.

Then, "It's Andy," Duncan told me. "He's really ill. That new doctor came to the Kullanders' place today. Alana told me. She – the doctor, I mean – she said she wouldn't recommend taking him to the mainland. She thinks he'll be happiest staying at home."

I warmed the teapot, thinking it over. "Well," I replied, "I think that's probably right, isn't it? He'll feel much better in his own home with his mam caring for him and you lot calling in on him – Fiona told me the doctor was going to visit. It's kind of her to come over from Storhaven when there's no real diagnosis. Reassuring for Fiona and Alf, I'm guessing."

"*Aja*, but Mam…" Duncan's eyes were brimming with tears again.

Malcolm took over. "The doctor doesn't think there's a cure," he explained.

"*Nei*, I know, but –" Then I realised what they were saying. "Is he very ill?" I gasped. "Is he…?"

"The doctor has suggested that his sister and brothers might want to come home, weather permitting – before the Solstice."

My heart was thumping hard in my ribcage. I was thinking of Fiona. Andy was her youngest child, and the one who had always needed her most. How must she be feeling? How would I feel if it were Duncan we were talking about? "My God!" I said, rather lamely. I poured the tea slowly. It was proper tea, not the dandelion concoction, so I added milk and passed the mugs across. Then I sat on one of the rocking chairs. "How certain was she – the doctor, I mean? Fiona told me that they've never known for sure what the problem is. And he's been ill before, hasn't he, when he was just a wee laddie? Quite a lot, if I remember rightly."

"*Aja*," Duncan agreed, "but never like this. Do you remember? He used to have a few days, maybe a week, when he'd just laze around and not want to play, and then one day he'd be back to normal! We just called them his *episodes*. But he's been getting worse and worse. And the doctor thinks she's seen this sort of thing before… She doesn't think it's hereditary; she thinks it's the result of some sort of pollution."

That didn't make sense to me. "Pollution?" I queried. "On En-Somi?"

"I know." Duncan was, I dare say, echoing my reaction. We had to be one of the least polluted places on earth. "But storms from across the Atlantic bring all sorts of particles… we learnt about it when I was still going to school on Shetland. And the oil and chemical industries…"

Malcolm stood up and took two steps across to the window. "She could be wrong," he pointed out, his back to us. "Didn't she say so herself?"

"Well," Duncan was being scrupulously honest, "I heard from Alana, and she heard from her mam, and her mam heard from Andy's mam, so it's difficult to know."

"Perhaps you should go up there and visit Fiona again?" Malcolm suggested to me.

"*Aja*," I agreed. "I could go first thing tomorrow. And do you think we should phone Verity and Lyle? So that we can hold the family in the Light?"

"Mam," Duncan asked, a little tentatively. "Will you show me how to do that? Hold people in the Light, I mean. Andy's my best friend – or he was, until I knew Marigold."

★★★

Of course, the whole of Gamla Hus had heard the news by the following morning. I called in at the shop on my way to Fiona's, and found Rose standing at the counter talking to Shona, while Alec stood whining and tugging at her jacket.

"I'm sorry!" Rose said to Shona and me. "He isn't usually grumpy like this, are you my laddie? But Thistle's spending the morning at the school – she's four now, you knows. Sigrid likes to start the wee ones off with a few hours in class, singing and playing with the others who are going to start school soon. She likes to break them in slowly. And Alec wanted to stay wiv 'er. They ain't 'ardly ever been parted before!" She bent down and hoisted her toddler onto her hip. "You'll be off to school with Thistle in no time!" she reassured her son.

Alec stopped whinging and put his thumb in his mouth. He was the sweetest little lad.

"'Ave you 'eard about Andy Kullander?" Rose asked. "Isn't it awful?"

"I don't remember Alana ever being so upset," Shona agreed. "Those bairns have been a foursome for years! And how Fiona and Alf must be feeling – I really can't imagine!"

"You saw Fiona after the doctor had been, didn't you?" I was remembering what Duncan had told me.

"*Aja*. She walked down the hill with Dr Emmylou – she had ridden over on her pony; – a funny sight, that! Such a tall doctor and such a small pony! Anyway, the doctor had stabled her pony at the *fi'ilsted* and walked up to the Kullander's place, so Fiona walked back down with her."

"How did she seem?" I wondered.

"It was hard to tell." Shona was wriggling her fingers at Alec, who was giggling, so that there was an odd contrast between the bairn's laughter and the terrible subject of our conversation. "Stoical, I would say," she added, smiling at the wee one.

"I'm going up there now," I said. "I've brought some blueberry muffins that Duncan made yesterday evening."

Rose was looking from one to the other of us. "It's odd," she told us. "I never thought what you would 'ave tragedies too, you *En-Som-in-Fedii*. It seemed to me what we used to be refugees and slaves, we was the ones what 'ad to cope with stuff like this…"

"I suppose sad things happen to everyone," I suggested. "But you did have it worse than most."

"Not now though," reassured Shona, who knew Rose well. "You're no more likely to suffer than everyone else, and if you had troubles, we would be with you." She tickled the wee laddie, who wasn't old enough to understand the gravity of our conversation. "Wouldn't we, young Alec? We'd be right here with you!"

Gales of laughter issued forth from the wee one and Rose smiled proudly at her son.

"Give them my love," she said. "If there's anything I can do…"

★★★

I found Fiona and Alf sitting on the stone bench outside their home. Alf leapt to his feet when he saw my head appear above the low wall of their patio – it's a steep climb up to the Kullander's place. He held my right hand warmly in both of his.

"Marie! Thank you for coming!"

Fiona remained seated. She looked white and drawn, which was not surprising.

"I'll make tea!" Alf offered, and went inside.

I sat next to Fiona. For a few minutes I said nothing. We were so still that a small brown bird settled briefly on the patio wall, pecked at something it found between the stones, and flew away again. From down in the village, we could hear the children playing outside, enjoying their morning break.

"I always thought this might happen," said Fiona, her voice tight and controlled. "He was never quite like my other bairns, right from the time he was born."

"He's special, all right," I agreed. "But not because of his illness." I paused. "I've been told grim stories," I added, "but all via the grapevine. How serious does the doctor think it is?"

Fiona sighed. "Well," she told me, "there isn't an actual diagnosis – you know that. So, she told me that her opinion is only two steps away from guesswork. She seemed pretty certain, though." Fiona was quiet for a minute or two. "She was very kind," she added. "She talked to Andy as if he were an adult, which is what he needed, and then afterwards she talked to me as if I were a child. And that was what I needed too!"

Alf came back with the tea. "If our bairns can get to Lerwick," he told Fiona, "we can book a helicopter to get them here. Cameron and Connell think they can make it, but Inger is still trying to make arrangements. There are dozens of road closures because of the last storm. But her Jimmy will get her to Aberdeen if it's humanly possible, and from there it shouldn't be too difficult…"

Fiona gave a little hiccup of grief, and for a moment her face crumpled. Then, apparently with great effort, she controlled herself. "Andy'll be pleased to see them," she commented, her voice almost harsh.

Alf leaned across me – we were sitting in a row with me in the middle – and put his hand on Fiona's knee. "You don't need to be brave with us," he chided her gently.

Fiona was very still. She gulped a couple of times and sipped her tea. Then, in that very controlled voice she explained, "If I start to cry now, I think I might never stop." She turned to look behind her and upwards, taking in the red-painted walls of the house. "Up there, there's a laddie who needs me. There'll be enough time for crying later!"

"Maybe a lot later," suggested Alf, sitting back.

"*Nei*, Alf, my love," Fiona responded. "Not this time, I fear. I don't think the laddie will see Solstice."

There was a silence after that. I reached out and held Fiona's hand, and she gripped it tightly. The little brown bird came again, looked at us with its head on one side and decided not to stay. Down in the village a cock crowed and a small sweep of gulls glided overhead, surfing the thermals, then turned and gracefully curved back towards the sea. The world looked beautiful but upstairs, if the doctor was right, an eighteen-year-old bairn was dying. Another blast of the terrible ones.

CHAPTER 8

There were more of us at the meeting that Sunday, which was, I suppose, not surprising. Malchi was there, leaving Petter to mind the *fi'ilsted*, and Duncan, Alana and Marigold arrived just as we all settled down. Alf came in and sat in the corner by the door, and about ten minutes in, Olaf appeared, leaning heavily on his stick.

About halfway through, there was a bit of a commotion and wee Thistle appeared in our midst, proclaiming loudly, "I wants Marigold to come and play with me!"

Marigold smiled apologetically at us all and left, shushing her little sister. A few minutes later, Verity came in. It turned out that Marigold had offered to look after their two bairns along with Thistle.

At one point, Lyle stood and recited again some of the words he had first read out to us the morning after Bonnie's birth. He only spoke the beginning of the quotation: *Thou hast been a strength to the poor, a strength to the needy in his distress.* In my head, I finished it: *a refuge from the storm, a shadow from the heat, when the blast of the terrible ones is as a storm against the wall.*

A few minutes later, Olaf stood creakily to his feet. "Oh, you who rule the heavens," he declared, "if you are there, help us in our distress!"

I heard Malchi murmur a subdued "Amen" and Alana sniffed, so that I realised that she was weeping.

Nobody stayed for tea at the end of the meeting, although I think Olaf and Alf went to the *fi'ilsted*.

★★★

We celebrate the two Solstices every year on En-Somi, but not the Equinoxes. Nevertheless, I know we are all aware of them. The end of September arrived and we had more hours of dusk and darkness than we had of daylight. The hot days of summer seemed like distant memories, and shorts and flip-flops were stored away until another uncharacteristically hot time should come to us. People began to think about pulling their little rowing boats, from which we all fished, up out of the water. Alf, Yanni, Eric (who lived – and still lives – in the new bothy the Kullanders built) and Si had done sterling work rebuilding the stonework of the summer harbour, a foot or more higher than the old quay. Sea levels had risen noticeably, and the flat surface where only a few years ago the bairns had burnt their wee houses in honour of the *huldufolk*, the hidden people, was now usually under water.

Over in Storhaven they were experiencing similar issues. Tom, the man who managed the port and whose bothy was right at the water's edge, had twice been flooded, and the *Oyrod* had approved the rebuilding of his home several feet back from the harbour wall, and higher. We heard that the sea had already breached the sand dunes over at St Matthew's Bay, which was surprising because the damage hadn't been done during a particularly rough storm or an unusually high tide. Mirren hadn't been able to recruit any help to defend the bay, and her concerns had obviously been justified.

Traditionally, the autumn has its own joys. Salted or dried fish are stored in barrels, potatoes buried in clamps, preserves of all sorts line the shelves of people's storehouses, and final repairs are done to bothies and outhouses before the winter storms blow in. Excitement among the bairns grows steadily as September turns to October, and they long for their mid-year tests to be over so that they can start to prepare for *Huldufolk* Day, Solstice and Christmas.

That autumn was rather subdued, it seemed to me. The three remaining bairns still met regularly in my bothy or at Alana's home, but they were quieter, less prone to playing pranks on each other or to teasing Marigold. They visited Andy regularly, although Duncan told me that as often as not he was asleep.

"And he's so thin," Marigold added. "And his eyes look all wrong."

The lad's three siblings, Cameron, Connell and Inger, arrived together, not by helicopter but on a ferry, which also brought crates of tinned goods and – wonder of wonders – coffee! Carefully packed in damp compost, Harry also found the apple saplings, looking rather sad after their journey, and not at all as if they might grow well and one day provide us with fresh fruit! We didn't see much of the Kullander family once they were all together; they seemed to have hunkered down in their own home, looking after each other. The doctor rode over regularly, always stabling her pony at the *fi'ilsted* and striding up the slope, past Oda's Corner where the ruined shrine still stands. I visited once or twice, but now that her daughter was there, it seemed to me that Fiona needed me less. There was, I recall, a sense of waiting in the air; a pausing of normal life.

It was during this time – I suppose sometime at the beginning of October – that I had an unexpected visit. Freya Munro had been to my bothy once before, during a time when the *bondii* had been struggling with the twin problems of high taxation and thefts from their storehouses. Freya was *harkrav*, and therefore one of the wealthier class of islanders, and lived in elegant surroundings on the east of the island, in the area known as Floirean's Cnoc. Since the day of that visit, years earlier than the events I'm describing now, I hadn't seen her. Blair Munro, her husband, no longer lived on En-Somi, but Magnus Munro had been one of the lads who had interrupted our meal so I assumed he was living with his mother and that she had not left with her husband. That was not surprising. There was, I knew, no love lost between them.

She arrived at my bothy without warning. In fact, it was lucky that I was in. We had a meeting of our knitting cooperative planned for lunchtime. I had to curb the thought that it was typical *harkrav* behaviour just to assume that I would be available when Freya Munro wanted to see me!

It was, I remember, a grey and blustery day. Duncan was up at Alana's and Malcolm was down on our beach, sorting out his boat and also looking for any useful driftwood which he and Petter could use to make beakers. My little bothy doesn't take much looking after. I seem to remember that I had swept the floor and made Duncan's bed, and was just thinking of settling down to a book that Elise's mam had recommended and which I had downloaded. Then there she was, simultaneously knocking on the door and opening it, without waiting for me to answer.

"Hello, Marie!" she greeted me, taking off a scarf that looked like silk, which she had been wearing to keep her hair immaculate in the wind. "I hope you don't mind me calling like this? I'm looking after the Fox-Drummin's ponies and they need exercising regularly. I've left them up where the track narrows. Do you think they'll be all right?"

I felt like saying something cutting – perhaps asking her if she had tied them up – but I swallowed my indignation and tried to put on a welcoming smile. "Tea?" I offered. "Coffee? We actually have some now that the ferry's called."

"Oh, tea, please," my visitor answered as she settled herself into one of my rocking chairs. "Do you have Earl Grey? If not, breakfast tea will do. Is the rest of your family out?"

"Duncan – my son – he's up in the village," I told her. "Malcolm's beach-combing."

"Oh well…" Fiona sounded slightly peeved, as if we had let her down by not all being at home. "Maybe you can help?" she asked.

I poured the tea (we didn't have the woman's chosen mix, so it was our normal fair-trade brand) and seated myself in the other rocking chair. I thought regretfully of the hour I had hoped to spend reading before the knitters met up, but then reminded myself that, after all, the book would wait. Here was a woman who wanted to talk about something, and although I couldn't say I was very fond of Fiona Munro, she was a guest in my house. "So, what's up?" I asked.

The woman looked away from me, staring out of my south-facing window. She sipped her tea, then looked around – perhaps hoping for an occasional table where she could place her mug. Finding no such thing, she continued to cradle it in both hands. "Did you know that my younger son, Magnus, is back on En-Somi?" she asked.

"*Aja*, I did," I told her. "In fact, I've seen him once, over here in Hus. Doesn't he look like his older brother?"

"I suppose he does." Fiona didn't sound proud or gratified that I had seen the similarity, the way I might have expected an island parent to respond. "He didn't get his place at Oxford," she told me. "The stupid boy rather blotted his copybook at school. You'd think they'd make allowances for normal teenage high jinks, wouldn't you? But you know, they let all sorts of people into universities nowadays. They're quick enough to make allowances for youth from poor neighbourhoods or who aren't white, but when it comes to a well-connected young man whose older brother acquitted himself with honour, they're not interested."

I wasn't sure what to say to that, so I gave a sort of grunt which Fiona could interpret as agreement if she so chose.

"So, he's taking a year out," the woman continued. She looked around again for the non-existent occasional table, then stood and took her empty mug to the kitchen sink. Returning to her seat, she continued, "He'll put it on his CV as voluntary work in a deprived community. I'll find someone to write him a good reference at the end of the year. But the boy needs to avoid contact with the police. They do background checks at universities now."

"Well, that shouldn't be too hard," I pointed out. "There're only two *nasyonii* on the island!"

"Mm, I know." Fiona looked, I thought, rather uncomfortable. "But my sons are high-spirited. We managed to keep that other incident quiet –"

I couldn't resist it. I interrupted with, "You mean when Magnus's brother beat up young Harris?"

The woman looked a bit shocked. "'Beat up' is putting it rather strongly!" she reprimanded me. "It was just a bit of a tiff. Everyone overreacted. I dare say the young man deserved it!"

We had all seen a good part of the attack on our phones at the time, so I knew that our gentle neighbour, Harris, had simply been looking out for two of our refugees, the young couple who were, by the time the events in this tale took place, living with Holti. The older Munro boy had been taunting the newcomers. The older Munro boy had just stood up for them. There was no point, though, in pointing that out to Fiona Munro, so I kept my peace.

"What voluntary work is Magnus doing?" I wondered. I had vague pictures in my head of the sort of things our young people had done in their summer holidays: working on the land, repairing tracks and dry-stone walls, even helping with shearing the sheep.

Fiona laughed. "Oh, he isn't actually *doing* anything!" she told me. "Well, not by way of voluntary work! We asked around when he first came back to the island in June, but nobody seemed to want Magnus working with them around their crofts – you *bondii* can be quite cliquish, you know! And that police officer – Mirren? She was looking for people to work over at St Matthew's Bay. They wanted to reinforce the dunes with rocks so that the sea didn't flood the old airport and spoil the land, but really, can you see my Magnus carrying rocks back and forth? It would have been like a scene from Robben Island!"

"I see," I replied, sounding non-committal. I was thinking that work like that might have done young Magnus quite a lot of good.

"The trouble is," Fiona Munro continued, "that since he hasn't found any work he really wants to do, he's just taken to hanging around with some local lads – and a girl – and I'm afraid they'll lead him into bad ways."

Personally, I thought it was more likely to be the other way round, but I kept that thought, along with the others, to myself. "How can I help?" I asked. "As far as I know, Magnus doesn't come to Hus. I've only seen him over here once, and that was during that very hot spell a couple of months ago. I don't think our bairns really know him."

Fiona was twisting that pretty silk scarf around in her hands. "You might be right about the lads," she agreed. "I mean, they might not come from this side of the island. I think there's a Stewart and a MacLoughlan youth from bothies over towards Frigg Moor – typical *bondii* with no ambitions beyond farming their fathers' land. But there's the girl, too… I dare say she's the source of all the trouble. And she's definitely from over on this side of the island."

I guessed at once that the lassie must be Elin, but what was this trouble Fiona was referring to? I wasn't sure how to phrase my question. "What are you worried about?" I asked. "What do you think they are up to?"

Fiona was still not looking at me. "Well, you know…" She paused. Then, when I didn't help her out, she said, "Alcohol, sex…" There was a long pause. "Drugs," she added. "That was the problem at school. And Magnus really can't afford to get a police record. These things always come back to haunt you, you know, even when they are just childish indiscretions!"

I thought about the container on the beach and my discussion about drugs with Duncan. I remembered the mention of 'shrooms' in Elin's song and her cry to me, when I had met her on the side of Fyrtarn Fjell, that her world, unlike mine, was not wholesome and good. "Perhaps you're right to be worried," I conceded. "Have you talked to Magnus? What does he say?"

The woman looked embarrassed. "The thing is, that when they were younger, when they came home for the school holidays, the boys heard how their father spoke to me…"

"Magnus is rude to you?" I prompted.

"He threatens me," Fiona answered in a very quiet voice.

"Ah." I was way out of my depth. "Do you have any friends on the island – maybe a male up on Floirean's Cnoc who your son respects? Maybe one of your neighbours would have a word with him?"

Fiona was quiet for a moment. "That's not how things work among us," she told me and I realised that she was referring to her fellow *harkrav*. "Blair would hate it if he knew that I hadn't kept up appearances. He's still paying maintenance, you see."

"I see." What could I say? I realised that this woman couldn't control her son and that it was probably not her fault, but another part of my brain, or maybe my heart, was screaming, *But what about Elin? Who's looking out for Elin?*

"So that's why I've come to you," my guest continued. "I'm sure it's that young girl who's causing all the trouble and, as I've told you, she definitely doesn't come from our side of the island. And I know your husband has authority over here. He's on the *Oyrod*, isn't he? So, I thought he might say something to the child. Or maybe your police officer might? You know, threaten her a bit? Warn her to stay away from people who are better than her?"

I couldn't believe what I was hearing! She wanted Malcolm or Lyle to *threaten* Elin? Was that how the *harkrav* thought you should manage troubled teenagers? And did Fiona Munro really believe that wee Elin was the source of her son's misbehaviour? A lassie who had probably never gone further than Shetland? And Magnus had already been in trouble at his expensive boarding school for something drug-related! I couldn't let it rest. "Why do you think Elin's to blame?" I wondered. "Surely your son is the one who knows all about drugs!"

"Ah! I thought you would guess who the girl is," Fiona told me, a little gleefully. "That more or less proves that you already know she's trouble! So don't you go blaming my son. He's just easily led!" She glared at me. "And I'll warn you now, if you don't do something about that chit, I'll make sure that we do. Blair knows people… I only have to drop a word in his ear!"

CHAPTER 9

Tom, down at the ferry port, had ordered a camera for Jarvis, our eccentric wild man who roamed the moors and clifftops. I don't know how it had come about, but Elise had taught him the rudiments of photography and was posting his pictures on a website that she had created. The bairns were aware of this development before me. Marigold showed me some of Jarvis's work on her phone.

"I can't think how he got so close to the puffins," she told me. "I know they're friendly little creatures, but look!" She was showing me a close-up photo of one of the little birds, its mouth full of sand eels. "Isn't that a good picture? And look at this –"

Her finger swept across the screen, past a couple of other photographs, and stopped at a picture of a blue hare, its coat still changing from its summer brown to winter snowy white, staring almost sternly into the camera lens as if confronting Jarvis with some irrefutable fact.

I took the phone from her and looked at the other pictures. They were lovely; she was right. Most were of the wildlife that lives on or around En-Somi, but a few were of landscapes. There was a long view from the top of Fyrtarn Fjell looking east, and another which I guessed must have been taken from the top of the cliffs over towards Hunger Moor, facing west.

Marigold was looking over my shoulder as I scanned the pictures. "He doesn't really like people," she commented. "But he seems to love nature – anything living and breathing! Anything that might need protecting."

"*Aja,*" I agreed, "but that does include some people. He tried to save Lavender when she was washed out to sea, didn't he? And he definitely wanted to protect you when he feared that social services would take you away from your mam and paps. And he's worried about Elin now."

Marigold was quiet for a few minutes. We were sitting in my bothy, waiting for Duncan to finish showering and dressing before the bairns went to visit Andy.

"Does he know where Elin is living?" she asked. "I'm worried about her, too. I know I said she was *felbilli*, but I think I was just being mean. She's a bit lost, really, isn't she? When I think of all the things Mam and I talk about, all the stuff she explained when she was expecting Alec – well, wouldn't it be strange not to have a mam to tell you those sorts of things? And Christian told me that even if her mam had been alive, she was a bit of a strange one. Christian doesn't remember her, but his *pari-pari* said she used to daydream in a way that nobody could wake her up from. Go into trances, stuff like that. And I might be wrong, but I can't imagine Fiona Munro looking after Elin like a real mam, even if she is Magnus's girlfriend."

"Elin mentioned something about her mam being a little unusual," I reflected. "She overheard someone saying her mother had been unbalanced and that she shouldn't really have had any bairns. And I'm sure you're right – Magnus's mam won't be any help at all to Elin." It didn't seem at all wise to tell Marigold of my conversation with Fiona Munro.

Marigold chuckled. "I think we're all a bit unbalanced if you really get down to it." Then she looked more serious. "But imagine growing up with that idea in your head. You'd wonder all the while whether you'd taken after your mam, wouldn't you? And you'd wonder if it might have been better if you'd never been born."

I wanted to tell Marigold what Bjorn had told me – that Elin's paps was grateful to have Elin – but, just at that moment,

Duncan appeared on the scene, his hair damp and tousled and a big grin on his face.

"If you're not careful," he pointed out, "you'll get into a nature versus nurture debate and then we'll be here all morning! Come on, Marigold – let's get going! Did you bring those biscuits you made?"

The two young people put on their shoes and coats, and waved a cheerful goodbye. As they left, I heard Marigold say, "Thistle's drawn a picture for Andy. Don't let me forget to give it to him!"

When they had left, teasing each other about something or other with great good humour, I was left wondering again – what exactly was going on with Elin? How could such a sweet child have made such a poor impression on Fiona Munro? And were we doing enough to help?

★★★

It was about that time – maybe a few days later, though it's hard to be sure, now that I'm so old – that Malcolm came in one afternoon and suggested we go for a walk. It was late in the afternoon. I remember that I had started making our evening meal. Duncan was probably still up in the village, doing whatever the youngsters did when they gathered in the meeting house at the end of their online lessons. It had been very windy earlier in the day, with dark, almost navy-blue clouds rolling over the island, threatening rain that didn't come, but the clouds were clearing and the wind had dropped a little.

Malcolm stood at the entrance to our bothy, still wearing his boots and the orange waterproof jacket he favoured when he was out in his boat. He looked, as always, a little scruffy. His hair needed trimming and his beard looked unkempt, and I felt a surge of love for him. "It's turned bonnie," he told me. "Let's walk up to the top of the cliffs – there's going to be a beautiful sunset."

We left a note for Duncan (although there was really no need) and set off. The first part of our walk was steep and there was no clear footpath, just sheep tracks which sometimes led nowhere. I went ahead, talking over my shoulder to my partner about insignificant things; I don't remember what. Probably a book I had been reading or my latest knitting project. When we reached the top of the hill close to where the puffins had nested, the track becomes more defined, and we walked arm-in-arm along the top of the cliff.

Malcolm was right. Up there, high above the rolling, crashing waves, the wind was strong and cold but the air was crystal clear, and everything seemed to be in sharp focus. Over towards the tiny, uninhabited island of Liten Stein, there were more of those heavy, black clouds, and the sun was low on the horizon, sometimes blocked out by the clouds and then, suddenly, gleaming brightly. Everything was dark green and navy blue, with streaks of gold and red and orange. Everywhere there were seabirds, swirling and crying into the wind, and the dark sea had white caps constantly churning and breaking on the surface. We stood close together, my arm round Malcolm's waist, his arm across my shoulders, but clumsily so because of our heavy outdoor wear.

"This must be where Jarvis was standing, that time when we were on the beach, and we thought he was going to jump. Do you remember?"

Of course I did. "We know him so much better now," I said. "I was quite frightened of him back then. Or wary, anyhow."

"*Aja*," Malcolm agreed. "Most people were. It's easy to feel scared of people who are different."

"He's got a heart of gold, though," I added.

We heard movement behind us, heavy breathing not coming easily, and then a head appeared, and a stooped body. We were not the only ones to think about coming to watch the sunset.

"Olaf!" Instinctively, Malcolm stepped forward to help the old man up onto the flat ground at the top of the cliff. He was a little breathless and was leaning heavily on his walking stick, but for such an old man he was doing very well.

"I see I'm not the only person to think that the view might be good this evening!" Olaf remarked.

"It's stunning, isn't it?" I agreed. The lower edge of the sun just dipped towards the horizon at that point and the sky over the clouds turned bright red. "We're so lucky!"

The old man was quiet for a few minutes. We all were. It is odd that during the day you are hardly aware of the movement of the sun, but just as it sets you can actually see it sink into the sea.

"I come up here to clear my head," Olaf told us. "Or maybe to clear my heart. I look at all this –" he nodded out to sea, "and it reminds me that I am so small; that my problems are so insignificant… I feel I'm tossing all more difficulties over the cliff. The universe can deal with them."

We were all silent again. Then, very gently, Malcolm asked, "And do you have difficulties just now?"

"Don't we all – always?" retorted Olaf. Then he added, "Actually, since you ask, I do. *Aja*. I have a broken heart. Not the way lads and lassies do, when they are making and breaking partnerships. My heart is an old man's broken heart. The death of a dream, the fear of failure, of years not passed wisely."

I wanted to say, *but you're the wisest person I know!* Yet somehow, I understood that it would be better to keep quiet. In silence, we watched the sun set below the horizon as the colours in the sky turned from red to orange, to narrow streaks of gold. We must have stood there together like that for several minutes, saying nothing. Then Olaf started to speak again.

"Wee Elin has left her father's bothy," he said. "He came home yesterday and she had gone. Her clothes have gone, the notebooks where she writes her songs, her tablet, her *langspil*. I love her like my own grandchild, but she's gone. She didn't leave a note." He sighed. "I was so sure she was to be our next bard, I thought I had seen it, but it seems not. And soon I will leave this island for another world and you'll be left with no one – no one to record our history; no one to remind us of what has gone before. And I fear I have just confused that beautiful wee bairn. She has grown up thinking her destiny was clear, but now... I've taken too much into my own hands and it's too late to put it right." Were there tears in his eyes or was it just the wind?

"Oh, Olaf!" I sympathised, and reached out to touch his arm. It seemed, though, that there was no point in saying anything more.

★★★

Duncan and Marigold had also heard that Elin had left. It seems all the bairns who met up at the end of the day at the meeting house had been discussing the news, with a mixture of scorn and surprise.

"They say she's gone off with Magnus Munro," Duncan told me. "I can't understand what she sees in him. He's just an arrogant –" He gulped. "Sorry, Mam, I was going to say something rude!"

Malcolm laughed. "I dare say you wouldn't have said anything your mam hasn't heard before!"

"She's very young to leave her paps' hearth, isn't she?" I commented. Elin was several years younger than my Duncan. "Aren't there laws about minors leaving home?"

"She's really just run away," Malcolm said. "You'd be surprised how often teenagers do that. They go for a few days and then they return home. I used to see it all the time! In fact, my Beth tried something along those lines once, after I put my foot down about something or other."

Duncan looked interested. "What happened?" he wondered.

Malcolm chuckled. "She said I was too strict – too protective, and that she was old enough to look after herself. And then she stormed out. I can tell you, I was worried sick until I knew where she was!"

"How long did she stay away?" I asked. I hadn't heard this story before. "Where did she go?"

Malcolm laughed again. "To her friend Moira's, three doors along from us," he told us. "Moira's mam phoned to tell me she was there, although we didn't tell the girls about the call. And Beth came home after school the next day, because she needed her gym clothes. And that was the end of it!"

"I think this business with Elin might be more serious than that," I suggested.

"*Aja*," Duncan agreed. "And, to be honest, none of us – those of us who go to the meeting house – are really surprised. I'm more upset about Andy. We went up to see him today – Alana, Marigold and I. Connell and Cameron were out with their paps, but Inger and Fiona were there, and we talked to them for a while. Inger was close to tears all the while. Andy can't keep his food down any more, so he's just fed on liquids. The doctor, Emmylou, she's shown Fiona how to make a healthy drink based on nettle tea. We tasted it – it's quite pleasant, actually. But they said that Andy isn't interested." He sighed. "Marigold was in tears on our way down to Hus. I asked her if she'd like to come here for supper, but she said she wanted to be with her mam. She said that helping to put the wee ones to bed was the best thing for taking her mind off other things."

"There seems to be a lot of sadness on our side of the island just now," Malcolm commented. "I can't imagine how the Kullanders must be feeling, and as for Elin's paps – and poor Olaf…"

"I think you ought to go and see Elin's father," I suggested to my partner. "He'll need to know that people are standing alongside him."

"*Aja*," Duncan agreed. "And to reassure him, too. I mean, Elin has left Gamla Hus but she's still on the island! She could come home any day. It isn't as if she's gone to Australia!"

"You're right," agreed Malcolm. "I'll go tomorrow. I'll take two of my new wooden beakers as an excuse!"

★★★

But he didn't. Fiona phoned in the early hours of the following morning. We hadn't put our phones on silent; I think we all knew that we might hear bad news at any time. I was awake first and clambered down to the table where we charged all our devices at night.

It was a WhatsApp message – bleak and abrupt: 'Andy died at 2.45, in his sleep.' I was just typing an ineffective reply – what can you say? – when Duncan's phone bleeped too. I took it across to his sleeping nook.

"Duncan! Duncan, my love, you've got a message from Alana."

He stirred and opened his eyes. "What?" Then I suppose he took in the expression on my face. He grabbed his phone and swiped it open. Alana must have heard the news from her mam and contacted her friends at once. I saw Duncan's face crumple. "Oh, Mam!" he blurted out, then turned away from me. His shoulders were shaking. He was not a child any more; he didn't want me to hug him – not yet, at any rate.

I rested a hand on his arm and let him cry. I was crying myself.

★★★

There wasn't a minister at the kirk by then. Verity was the last person on En-Somi to have that role. The Kullanders were definite, however, about the arrangements they wanted to mark the end of Andy's life. There was to be a simple burial service up on Aeloff's Hill where the island cemetery has served us for centuries and then a meeting for remembering Andy in our meeting house a day or two after that.

Fiona told me later that they had expected the actual burial to be a small affair. Aeloff's Hill is right across the island from Gamla Hus – you have to go to Storhaven and then follow the track north towards St Matthew's Bay; a three-hour journey if you're walking, but, of course, much quicker in a pony-drawn cart. As it turned out, she was wrong. Quite a few *En-Som-in-Fedii* made their way over to the east of the island and stayed with family and friends the night before the ceremony, and Robert and Malcolm both took full cartloads of villagers when we drove over.

For Rose and Si it was a strange experience. Their daughter Lavender, the one who had been swept out to sea, was buried in that cemetery, and although they had a photo of the grave fixed onto one wall of their bothy, they had never been there in person. The wee ones, Thistle and Alec, only knew of Lavender from the tales the family told, but Marigold had been close to her sister and still missed her, she confided to me.

It was a wild, blustery day. Verity had agreed to lead the simple ceremony. Fiona and Alf were not, at that time, particularly concerned about religion, although both believed that there was some sort of life after death. I think Cameron – or it might have been Connell – had flirted with the Wee Frees, so they wanted something vaguely religious to take place, but only a few of us knew many hymns or appropriate songs. Verity assured the Kullanders that they needn't worry. Andy would be laid to rest with due solemnity. "And with love," she told them.

We were to meet at the cemetery at midday. Malcolm and I had a full cart, with all of Marigold's family and Duncan squeezed in as best we could manage. Wee Thistle, who looked more and more like Marigold as she turned from a preschooler to a bairn who could count to ten (most of the time) and who, like her big sister, asked endless questions, insisted on sitting at the front with Malcolm and her paps. It followed, of course, that Alec had to join them. The rest of us had quite a cheerful ride over despite Duncan being rather subdued and Marigold being torn between memories of her last journey across the island and thoughts about her dead friend. We had all put away our summer clothes, and the bairns looked colourful in their bright winter jackets and woollen hats although we adults were wearing darker shades in honour of the occasion. The clouds were low and the wind was blowing from the south, so that the Fyrtarn Fjell pass was very blustery and the wind swept across the open moor where the ruined chapel was slowly falling down.

A small crowd had already gathered when we arrived. Tom from the ferry port was with a group of Storhaven folk I had seen in The Castle *fi'ilsted*. Mirren, the Storhaven *nasyoni*, was talking to Holti, and Mo and Quincy were standing a little apart, looking out to sea. They seemed to have changed a lot since I had last seen them. Mo and Quincy no longer looked like teenage dropouts, instead they resembled any young island couple. And Holti, who had so often looked dishevelled and a bit confused, looked smart and, I thought, younger. I realised that it must be suiting those three to live together. The family who lived in the new bothy built on Kullander land was there, of course. They had lived with Fiona and Alf for months, and had probably known Andy better than any of the others who had once been refugees, except Marigold.

Marigold took her family to see Lavender's grave as soon as we arrived. It was neat and tidy, with the letter 'L' and a heart marked out in pebbles, and an old beer bottle wedged between some rocks containing a bunch of winter heather.

"I bet Jarvis did that," commented Duncan quietly to me.

"I think so," I agreed. "Bless him!"

Thistle was old enough to realise that the occasion was serious. Although she had no memories of Lavender, she stood beside the kneeling Rose at the graveside and said, "Love you, Lavender!"

Alec didn't grasp what was happening. He ran round the graveyard imitating his sister, calling, "Love oo, Lavvy!" His cries getting louder and louder, until Si picked him up and carried him to the cemetery wall, saying, "Let's see if we can see any boats, shall we?"

Verity and Lyle had stayed overnight at the Frasers' in Storhaven, and left their little ones with Ingrid so that Verity was free to concentrate on the funeral. We were all there – at least thirty of us, I would say – when Alf's cart arrived. Fiona and Alf were sitting at the front with Inger between them, and Andy's two brothers were in the back with the body of Andy, wrapped in a white cloth in the manner of *En-Som-in-Fedii*. A hole had already been dug in the peaty earth and we stood sombrely around it.

Verity stood at the head of the grave. Her voice was clear and strong as she recited a few words, mostly from the Bible: *God shall wipe away all tears from their eyes; and there shall be no more death, neither sorrow, nor crying, neither shall there be any more pain: for the former things are passed away. Fear not, for I am with you; be not dismayed, for I am your God; I will strengthen you, I will help you, I will uphold you with my righteous right hand... Blessed are they that mourn: for they shall be comforted... whether or not it is clear to you, no doubt the universe is unfolding as it should. Therefore, be at peace with God...*

She didn't say any formal prayers, but simply asked us to stand in silence, to reach out in our hearts to the Spirit who lives and works in all things, and to give thanks for the lad we had known and loved. Then she gave a little nod to Cameron and Connell, who lifted Andy's body gently into the grave.

Everything went quiet. In the distance, we could hear all the usual, homely sounds of En-Somi: waves breaking, sheep baaing, gulls calling... And then, suddenly, drifting across the moving air from just beyond the cemetery, the sound of music – a beautiful, sad voice and the gentle tones of a *langspil*. The words were clear and entirely new to me:

Cry, gulls, as you rush and sweep,
Plunge, you orcas in the deep,
Scatter you snow hares, run and leap,
And cry, my eyes, for the one who has gone.

Blow, winds, across the moors,
Rattle the shutters, hammer on the doors,
Beat the waves against the shores,
And choke my voice for the one who has gone.

Rumble, thunder, roll and crash,
Strike, lightning, pierce and flash,
Pour down rain with beat and lash,
And darken my mind for the one who has gone.

Churn, seas, break and foam,
Crash to shore, surge to home,
Swamp the light, kill the flame,
And cry, my heart, for the one who has gone!

The song finished and we stayed there, in silence. Tears were pouring down Fiona's face. Duncan had his arm around Marigold. Verity and Lyle were holding hands. It was the saddest song I had ever heard, full of sorrow and pain, but utterly beautiful. And we were all looking in the same direction. Just beyond the cemetery wall, Elin had been sitting on a rock, finishing the ceremony in a more glorious, more heartbreaking way than anything we could have imagined. We saw her stand. For a moment, she just looked at us, people she had known most of her life. People she had left. Then she turned and walked away.

"Was that a' angel?" Thistle asked Marigold in a hushed tone.

"I don't know," Marigold answered, with a catch in her voice.

CHAPTER 10

Malcolm, Duncan and I stayed up late that night. We sat around the warm glow of my heater, listening to the creak of the wind turbine and the occasional clatter of sleet against the shutters. Malcolm and I were each nursing a whisky. We had offered some to Duncan, but he never did develop a taste for it, even many years later; he was drinking tea.

"It nearly broke my heart, that song," Malcolm commented.

"*Aja*, and then wee Thistle's question…" Duncan was sitting on the floor at my feet, his arms wrapped around his long legs. He no longer looked grief-stricken, just pensive. "Andy would have loved it," he added.

"She has such a gift," I agreed. "And just to turn up like that…"

"Where is she living now?" Malcolm's question was directed to Duncan.

"I don't know." Duncan looked sad again. "With that Magnus, I suppose. I wish she would come home."

"Isn't there something we can do about it?" I wondered. "I mean, she's only thirteen. What would you have done, Malcolm, when you were working?"

"Oh… Well, that's a different matter," my partner answered. "There's the law and good practice and safeguarding to think about in these situations. I suppose we would have tracked the wee lassie down and she might have gone into care, and if the laddie, who's over eighteen, had taken advantage of her –"

"Which I bet he has!" interjected Duncan.

"*Aja*, well, in that case he might have been prosecuted. But that was in Edinburgh. We're on En-Somi now."

"How can that make a difference?" I was indignant. "She's just a child, Malcolm! Think of Marigold a year or two ago! Think of your Beth when she was that age!" I love Malcolm's calm approach to life, but sometimes it can be a little frustrating.

"Well," he reminded me, "there are several differences. The same laws apply here, at least as far as protecting children goes, but there aren't any agencies to enforce them."

"There's the *nasyonii*," I pointed out, but even as I said it, I realised that I didn't know what Lyle or Mirren could do.

"*Aja*, indeed there is," Malcolm agreed. "And I know that Elin's father has spoken to Lyle. But what can they do? Do you think that if Lyle went over to Floirean's Cnoc and tried to retrieve Elin from the Munro household, it would do any good? Wouldn't he just drive her further away?"

We were all quiet.

"To be honest," Malcolm added, "with the best will in the world, and with all the agencies performing as they should, it hardly ever worked in Edinburgh either. Remember the fears Jarvis expressed? By the time a thirteen-year-old has run away from home and is living with her older boyfriend, so much water has already passed under the bridge…"

"But we can't give up on her!" I exclaimed.

"*Nei*, my love," Malcolm agreed. "We can't. But we need to do this – whatever we do – the right way. Elin is thirteen. She has her whole life ahead of her. We need to go gently."

"What's with all this 'we' business?" Duncan asked. "Does Lyle want you to help?"

"Maybe," Malcolm told him. "I'm not sure, but Elin's father does. And that is no small thing."

★★★

Olaf hadn't been at the burial, but he was there for the thanksgiving in the meeting house. The room was packed. The smaller bairns hadn't known Andy but their parents had, and as they wanted to be there, it was inevitable that quite a few little ones turned up. People stood and paid tribute to Andy – to his gentle, kind spirit; to his grasp of local dialect; to his acceptance of the illness that he had lived with all his life. Duncan told a funny story about Andy's total failure in the bread-making department, and one of the tutors from the online school had sent in a few lines appreciating his work ethic, and especially his enquiring mind. There was laughter when Alf described his son's first attempts at milking a goat, and tears when Ingrid told of sitting by his bed the night he died, holding his hand and singing island songs that Andy had known all his life. Sigrid had taught the primary school children 'The Parting Glass' and Olaf accompanied them on his *langspil*. The wee ones sang it through once, their high, childish voices sounding sweet and sad; then everyone joined in as we sang it a second time. I glanced towards Duncan when we got to the lines: *'Of all the comrades that e'er I had / They're sorry for my going away'*. He was standing with Alana and Marigold and several others of our teenagers. I saw that they had all joined hands and were singing together, their eyes closed. Most of them had tears rolling down their cheeks, but they were not alone in that.

When the song had finished, we all stood, many still with closed eyes. Then Olaf took the lead, as was the task of our bard.

"*En-Som-in-Fedii,*" he began, his voice slightly shaky. "Dear fellow islanders, this is a strange and a sad day. We have lost a lad from among us, but we will never forget him. He will live in our hearts and his body is released into the universe forever. But his soul – his soul is indestructible. Andy was a gift to us, a gift to his family and a gift to his friends. Let us always remember him with thanksgiving."

For a moment there was silence, then he continued.

"*En-Som-in-Fedii,*" he continued, "there are mysteries in the world which we cannot begin to grasp, beauties which we cannot comprehend. The endless variation of clouds, the songs of birds, the tiny flowers that grow between the rocks, the music of the burn – all these things are around us every day, and so often we do not see or hear them. There is a love, a creativity in nature, a goodness that has nothing to do with morality and everything to do with grace and glory. Andy is no longer here with us, but he is part of that grace and glory now. He has truly gone to a better place.

"And now it falls to us to fulfil the words of the song we have just sung, as if it were Andy himself telling us that it had *fallen to his lot that he should go and we should not. So let us fill the parting glass and drink a health what e'er befalls, then gently rise and softly call, good night and joy be to you all.*" Suddenly, his face lit up with one of his inimitable smiles. "In other words, fellow islanders, we will move on now to the *fi'ilsted*, where not only are there parting glasses available – or beakers, at any rate – but also food for one and all!"

CHAPTER 11

Mirren and Lyle, our two *nasyonii*, came to our bothy a day or so later. Unlike Freya Munro, they had checked that it was convenient in advance, so Duncan had headed up to Alana's to study, and Malcolm was whittling beakers from driftwood on the porch. It was a blustery day, with cold rain in the wind and with gulls wheeling and swooping over the white-flecked ocean. I was sorting out wool and knitting patterns, making a list of the colours I wanted for my next project. Neither officer was in uniform. They were chuckling about something when they arrived and were obviously on good terms. We four sat inside with rain splattering at intervals on the west-facing windows and talked a little about the death of Andy Kullander.

"I've spoken to the doctor," Mirren told us. "There were some formalities to do with the death certificate, but they're all ironed out now. She still believes that these new wasting diseases, as well as the huge rise in cancers, are the result of pollution. Haven't we all used non-stick pans and furnished our homes with fire-retardant fabrics? To say nothing of all the particles in the air and the microplastics in the sea…"

"It's surprising more of us aren't ill," commented Malcolm.

"*Aja.*" Lyle was thoughtful. "Verity and I are hoping that the next generation will be less vulnerable, now that the world is waking up to these things."

"I wonder," remarked Mirren, and I realised that she didn't take an optimistic view of the future. She cleared her throat, and turned to look directly at Malcolm and me, seated on the settle. "We can't do anything about environmental degradation right now, but there's a wee bairn we might be able to help. Elin. We've talked to various experts on the mainland and an officer in Shetland who has dealt with something like this before. They're generous with their advice, but with two huge storms shadowing the jet stream and coming in our direction, nobody wants to send a specialist over to En-Somi to help us."

I must admit, I felt rather relieved. I had once heard Jarvis talk about his experience in the hands of various agencies who certainly had only intended the best for him. It had been a pretty grim way to grow up. I had been shocked, too, when Malcolm had told me that if Elin had lived on the mainland, she might have been taken away from her father. On the other hand, Elin needed some sort of help.

"I've been over to Floirean's Cnoc," the *nasyoni* continued. "I had heard the suggestion that Elin might be living with the Munros." She stared out at the dark, stormy clouds for a moment, apparently collecting her thoughts. "I didn't get very far. Mrs Munro wouldn't let me in, so our conversation had to take place on her rather windy patio. And she would neither confirm nor deny that her son, Magnus, lived with her. The only information I was able to glean was that she despises young Elin. She called her several things I wouldn't want to repeat. She wanted me to find and arrest the bairn on unspecified charges."

"She came here, you know," Malcolm told Mirren. "She talked to Marie – she hoped we could separate her son and Elin."

"Aye, so I heard," replied Mirren. "That's really why we're approaching you. Lyle tells me that Elin has been here, to your home. She's friends with your son, isn't she? And Mrs Munro asked you for assistance. We don't think that either of them trusts us, so we wondered if you might be able to help?"

"Elin's never really been friends with Duncan," I clarified. "She did come here on one occasion, it's true, but it wasn't a success. Still, I'm fond of Elin. She confided in me once, just briefly… And you're right: Freya Munro has been here a couple of times; the last time was just a short while ago."

"I've known Elin since she was just a wee thing," Lyle added and I remembered when, many years earlier, Lyle had brought a couple of bairns to my bothy after a storm to check that all was well with me. Elin had been one of them. I felt a wave of grief as I thought of that small, vulnerable lassie and what might be happening to her. "But she's a teenager now. I fear I'm the bad guy."

"*Nei!*" Malcolm had been listening attentively. "We're none of us the bad guys. We're talking about a bairn, a confused and troubled wee thing who is probably in over her head. We need to take our feelings right out of the equation – even our suspicions about what she thinks of us. It's really important that we're clear-headed if we're going to achieve anything."

"What do we want to achieve, exactly?" I asked. "I mean, I can guess, but let's be specific!"

"Right!" Mirren smiled at me. "Our first aim is to get that child somewhere safe. To do that we need to know – for sure – where she's living now, and the circumstances of her present home life."

"You mean, is she sleeping with Magnus?" Malcolm asked.

"*Aja*," agreed Lyle. "But not just that. Are there drugs in the picture? There seem to be a few indications that there might be. Well, you know that – it was you who reported finding the magic mushrooms on the beach! And is the bairn staying away from home of her own free will, or is there an element of coercion?"

"And we need to know," added Mirren, "whether something happened at home to cause the wee lassie to run away. You all know Elin's father, and I dare say it's hard to think that he might be the root cause of these problems, but we mustn't rule anything out."

"Olaf has been to see me," Lyle added. "He's convinced he put too much pressure on Elin and that all of this is his fault. I have to say, I don't believe that – everything I saw told me that Elin loved being taught by Olaf and he's always been scrupulously careful about where he gave Elin her lessons. They were often in the school at the end of the day, and usually Sigrid was around... But Olaf is fretting."

"We don't need to question him or anything," Mirren explained. "But we feel we ought to keep him in the loop. As if he were a family member. Then," Mirren continued, "when we know a bit more about Elin's circumstances, we'll be in a position to know what to do next. After all, we could find out that she's safe somewhere, not being coerced or abused, just dealing with some teenage angst before returning home, older and wiser!"

"We could," agreed Malcolm, "but I'd be surprised. I haven't taken a liking to that Munro boy!"

★★★

The first thing I needed to do, if I was to help in this situation, was to visit Freya Munro. I really didn't want to, but I reminded myself that this was about Elin and not me.

Malcolm drove me over and dropped me off at the foot of the well-kept track that led up to the Munro bothy. We had agreed that he would keep out of sight so as not to worry Freya. I had texted her in advance, asking if I could visit, but she hadn't replied, so I wasn't a hundred per cent sure she knew I was on my way.

There was a fancy door-knocker on the door, made to look like a dolphin. I rapped on it and waited. I could hear Malcolm's ponies shifting in their harnesses at the bottom of the track, and there must have been chickens somewhere behind the building because I could hear their casual squawking conversations. Then the door opened and Freya Munro was standing there, glaring at me.

"I hope you've come to tell me that you've caught that silly girl and taken her to somewhere where she can't do any harm!" were her opening words. "But I don't suppose you have!"

"*Nei*, I'm afraid not," I answered. "Can I come in? I'd like to talk about the situation."

She opened the door wider and I found myself in a long stone-flagged room. At one end was an ultra-modern kitchen. The traditional small bothy windows had been enlarged and a dining table stood next to one, so that anyone sitting there could look out across the moors to the sea. There were sofas such as you might see in a Swedish style magazine. At the far end of the room there were two doors. I guessed they must lead to bedrooms and, presumably, a bathroom. The living area was about the size of a whole traditional En-Somi bothy, so I knew it must have been extended.

Freya led me to the seating area. "Do sit down," she invited, but she didn't offer me tea.

I sank into the sofa she had indicated. At once, it made me feel at a disadvantage. The furniture was designed in such a way that I found myself leaning back into the soft cushions. I shuffled forward so that I was more upright, perching on the edge of the seat, but all the while I was feeling clumsy, out of my element.

Freya sat sideways to me and crossed her legs in an elegant fashion. "So, what have you got to tell me?"

"I'm afraid very little at this point," I told her. "The *nasyonii* need to find out where the child is living. We wondered whether you had any ideas about that? Maybe Magnus might have mentioned something?"

"Huh! Not much chance of that!" the woman replied. "He doesn't tell me anything now that he's under the spell of that little hussy!"

I remembered things Freya had told me in the past. I was pretty sure that any meaningful relationship between mother and son had broken down years earlier. I asked, "So can you tell me when you first noticed a change in Magnus?"

The woman had the grace to look a little ashamed. "Well, you know, things were never that good between us. He grew up quickly – going to boarding school does that, but I dare say it's worth it. It makes them more independent. Self-reliant."

"And he came back to En-Somi – when?" I asked. "Presumably at the end of term? June? July?"

Freya gave a little cough, and looked away from me. "Well, no," she corrected me. "He had to leave school in May, right after he finished his exams. He went to his father's in Edinburgh for a few weeks, but his father – well, his father thought it might be better if he came here. I suppose it was in the middle of June that he arrived. Maybe a little earlier."

"And I think you told me that he was looking for work? Something voluntary that would look good on his CV?"

"Well, yes," agreed the woman. "But, honestly, I didn't believe it would ever happen. If the school couldn't manage him and his father couldn't control him, what chance did I have?" She looked across at me then. "Marie," she told me, "you don't know how lucky you are! Your son is so placid and biddable. I dare say it's his *bondi* genes – I've noticed before how stolid the island children are! My sons are – oh, I don't know! Sensitive! Easily spooked. Like racehorses!"

I tried to swallow my anger. Did the woman have any idea how insulting her comments were? So, Duncan was stolid, was he? And Freya's sons were like racehorses? She might as well have come straight out with it and said that we *bondii* were country bumpkins and the *harkrav* were pure-blooded. Aristocratic, even. But then I thought of Elin, and of the reason I was there. I suddenly remembered the phrase 'the blast of the terrible ones'. That was what all this was about. It concerned troubles and traumas that we felt we couldn't handle. And it was Elin who was in the direct line of those blasts right now. Any discomfort I felt at Freya Munro's tactless and self-centred comments was merely the slight breeze on the edge of the hurricane. "I am fortunate with Duncan," I managed to say. "He's a good lad. So, Magnus moved in with you. I suppose he's still living here?"

"Well, of course!" Freya exclaimed. Then she modified her statement. "In theory, at any rate."

Ah! I thought. *Now we're getting somewhere.* "But he isn't here just now?" I asked.

"Well, no." I thought the woman looked uncomfortable again. "He's made friends on the island. He spends a lot of time with them. He's not a child any more, you know! I don't need to keep track of his every movement!" Then she rallied. "But what has this got to do with anything? My son isn't the problem. It's that Elin. It's her you ought to be worrying about. The little tart!"

"Have you met Elin?" I asked.

"Briefly," the woman responded. "She was all lanky hair and black eye make-up. Every mother's worst fears! The daughter of a mad-woman, I gather. You can see it in her."

"She's very gifted." I felt I needed to stand up for the bairn. "She wrote and sang the most amazing song at Andy Kullander's burial."

"I dare say!" Freya Munro was clearly not impressed.

I realised that I still hadn't discovered any of the details I was supposed to be finding out. The woman seemed to be very good at fending me off. "So, Elin isn't staying here?" I asked.

"Good heavens, no!" Freya did actually look quite shocked. "Magnus knows better than to try that one on me! And can you imagine what Magnus's father would say if he heard that I had allowed that little trollop into my house!"

I decided to try another tack. "Magnus obviously knows that you don't approve of Elin," I suggested. "Do you think he's still seeing her?"

"God only knows!" She stood up and walked over to one of

those enlarged, east-facing windows, so that her next words were spoken with her back to me. "I'm sure he is still in touch with her. What red-blooded boy wouldn't be interested in a pretty little thing who puts it about! I dare say half the island youths follow her around!"

I was finding the conversation very hard. The Elin who Freya was talking about sounded so different from the Elin we knew. I thought of the bairn as young, lost, confused. Freya obviously thought she was promiscuous and out of control. Was it possible that I was wrong? And, I realised, I had still learnt no actual facts. I didn't know where Elin was, and I hadn't even discovered where Magnus was living.

Freya turned away from the window, but remained standing. "Look," she said, "I'm sure you no more approve of the behaviour of this chit than I do. All I want is for you to remove her from Magnus. That boy needs to have a quiet year here, no trouble with the authorities, no unfortunate situations, then he'll be off to university and out of my hair – and yours. So, can you just do that, please? Just – oh, I don't know! Tether her over on your side of the island? Send her to family in Shetland? I'm sure we could help with the cost, if that's the issue! But don't let her ruin my son's life!"

★★★

Mirren, Lyle, Malcolm and I were having lunch at The Castle *fi'ilsted*.

"It's no good trying to get information out of Freya Munro," I told them. "Somehow, she turned all my questions into tirades against Elin. But I definitely got the impression that Magnus isn't actually living with his mam."

"So that means we don't know where either of them is," Malcolm pointed out.

"*Nei*, and we don't actually know that they're together," Lyle pointed out. "Mirren, do we know for sure that they're not with those other lads – the ones who came over to Hus with Magnus in the summer?"

"Oh, aye, that's one thing we do know," Mirren responded. "I've visited their bothies and spoken to the parents. I've warned them that Magnus is no good. It was easy enough to convince the adults of that – they have no time for the *harkrav* – but the lads seemed quite enamoured with Magnus. And with Elin. The MacLoughlan boy showed me some video of Elin singing, some song about a hot summer. I could see why he was impressed. But his father is sending him back to Shetland on the next ferry. The Stewart lad hadn't told his folk that he knew Magnus. If I read the situation right, that lad is going to have a very watchful eye trained on him."

"And they didn't know where Elin or Magnus were living?" I checked.

"No," Mirren assured me. "They seemed to think that both were living at home – Magnus on Floirean's Cnoc and Elin in Hus."

"And the other lads who were with Magnus when they came over to the village?" Malcolm was ruling out any possibilities that came into his mind.

"Just hangers-on," Mirren told us. "One was an island Murray, the other – I'm not sure. A cousin to the island Murray, anyhow. They had both been uncomfortable about the events of that evening and haven't had anything further to do with Magnus. They were both followers of Elin online, though. But I don't think that helps."

We were all quiet for a moment, surveying the empty dishes left over from lunch.

"So, we're not that much further forward?" I asked.

"We are a bit." Malcolm sounded thoughtful. "At least we know of a few places where Elin isn't, even if we don't know where she is!"

"She's somewhere on En-Somi, still," I pointed out. "There hasn't been a ferry since Andy's burial."

"Who knows this island really well?" Mirren, who was a relative newcomer, asked. "Who would have an idea about where a couple of kids might hang out?"

And then we all realised. "Jarvis!" exclaimed Malcolm, Lyle and I in unison, and then we laughed. Of course, if anyone would know, it would be Jarvis!

CHAPTER 12

One of the reasons for the development of two communities on En-Somi, you should understand, is that until very recently (by the standards of so-called developed countries) we had very poor communications. Life had changed very little from pre-industrial times until the beginning of the twenty-first century, when the *harkrav* – who more or less ruled the island at that time – introduced wind turbines, ground and air source heating systems and the internet. We all realised that they didn't encourage these innovations to benefit us, the *bondii*. They hoped to develop the island as a tourist resort, capitalising on our remoteness and our 'quaintness' – the fact that we didn't use mechanised transport, for instance.

They were late to the game, however. Taking a wider view of things – and, of course – with the wisdom of hindsight, it's easy to see that many of the wealthy and the elite the world over refused to believe that climate change was a reality, and that the consequences would be dire even for them. By the time the little airport over on St Matthew's Bay had been built and a few bothies converted to holiday lets, the market for remote or 'wild' holidays was dying. Even transport systems on the mainland had become less reliable, and booking a trip to a place as remote as En-Somi was too great a gamble when storms were playing such havoc with flights and ferries, and when travel insurance had become almost impossible to obtain.

The *harkrav* themselves, of course, benefited from the developments they had introduced. Their homes in and around

Floirean's Cnoc became more than just addresses where they could register their fortunes for tax purposes. They became places where families could retreat from the growing instability and discomfort of a world where systems were breaking down and life was becoming more and more unpredictable. When I first came to En-Somi, a university dropout, newly married and pregnant with Duncan, more people were leaving the island than settling on it. The *harkrav* treated their lavishly-renovated or newly-built bothies as holiday homes. They were to be seen around in the summers and often made an appearance to witness our winter celebrations of *Huldufolk* Day and Solstice, and then stayed for Christmas.

At the time I am telling you about now, however, a few members of the *harkrav* were making En-Somi their permanent residence. They still sent their bairns to expensive boarding schools on the mainland, and several members of that tribe were definitely well-paid company directors of businesses which operated out of Edinburgh, London, Oslo or New York, but increasingly they worked from home, and 'home' was En-Somi.

The advantages to us, the *bondii* on the island, of all the technology that had been introduced was immense, even though it was largely accidental. In the space of just a few years, we were able to heat and power our homes with our own electricity and contact each other and the wider world via the internet. We could watch television for the first time, we could be on social media, but most of all, we could communicate with every part of En-Somi using our various devices. For a short while, just as I arrived on the island, we had that situation which is probably not so unusual in other parts of the world, where parents grew up with fish-oil lamps, turf fires and occasional community celebrations where they could catch up with family and friends, and their youngsters were at home with twenty-first century technology and almost unceasing communications. The transition was rapid and, by and large, welcome.

The *nasyonii*, Malcolm and I had briefly wondered about putting out some sort of plea to all *En-Som-in-Fedii* for information about where Elin might be living, but no sooner had we thought of it than we realised that such a message would probably just make matters worse. We thought it probable that Elin would shy away from us, and we knew that Magnus wanted nothing to do with the forces of law and order. The only really sensible thing to do was to revert to the idea we had first had when we were together at The Castle *fi'ilsted*, and try to make contact with Jarvis.

"Isn't he still living in the ruined airport?" Duncan asked over dinner, when we had been discussing the problem. "Why don't you go over and see him?"

"I think that's where we'll need to start," agreed Malcolm. "But he's all over the island nowadays. The last photos Elise posted on the website she created for him were taken down at our summer harbour."

"*Aja.*" I had been looking at the pictures just a few minutes earlier. "A white-tailed eagle just in the act of diving for fish. He's really such a gifted photographer!"

Duncan chuckled. "Hopeless with technology, though. Elise told me that he just brings the camera to her and asks her to upload the pictures. He doesn't even want to know how it's done!"

"Well then," I asked, "when shall we go over to St Matthew's Bay?"

"The sooner, the better," Duncan said. "I hate to think of wee Elin with that Magnus character! And there's two huge storms on the way. But I won't come, if you don't mind. I really want to revise for my exams."

***

It was a stunningly beautiful day, I remember. Although the forecast for the coming week suggested that the unusually pleasant weather wouldn't last, when we opened my bothy door and shutters just after sunrise at about 8 am, the sky was brightening to a clear, light winter blue and the breeze was gentle. Malcolm and Duncan had built stabling for his ponies at my place by then, although we still kept the cart in a little lean-to part way up to the village. We only widened the track down to my bothy a year or two after these events.

"Do you remember," Malcolm asked as we each led one pony up the narrow path, "the first few times we went over to St Matthew's Bay? How we always tried to take things over for the refugees? And how shy of me you were?"

I laughed. "Well, not *shy*!" I corrected him. "Cautious. I felt I was getting into something, but I didn't know what."

"I guessed almost as soon as I met you," he told me as we reached the lean-to and started to harness the ponies. "But I knew I had to go carefully. You seemed like a woman who didn't need anyone – or, at least, you didn't need another man in your life."

"It's true," I agreed. "I felt perfectly content. But now, looking back on it, I realise that it was exactly that – contentment, I mean. But perhaps I was not fully alive?"

"And now?" Malcolm was pushing for compliments.

"Now I never get any peace!" I answered. But I was thinking, *Then I was content. Now I'm happy – deep down, from the soles of my feet to the top of my head, I feel joy.*

Malcolm grinned at me. "That's what I thought," he said, climbing into the cart and reaching down to help me up. "You regret the moment you met me!"

Then, for a moment, he held me close, my face against his scruffy beard, and then kissed me. Even 'joy' wasn't a strong enough word to describe how I felt.

★★★

People on En-Somi don't really go on holiday. It's not because of climate change, although that has made even visiting family on Shetland trickier than it used to be. We were a very settled people even before all the more recent troubles. Our routines are tied to the land and the sea, to our families and our bothies – there is never a good time to be away.

Nevertheless, that morning it did feel the way I suppose other people must feel as they go on holiday: people on the mainland, for instance, or the *harkrav*. We had packed a lunch; we were going to see a man who, though strange, was a friend of ours; and in the meantime it was just the two of us, the ponies, the gulls, the rocks and the turf, and the perpetual, comforting sounds of the sea. Up on Fyrtarn Fjell the view was stunning. We looked behind us, and way on the horizon we both thought we could see the grey shadow of land.

"Maybe you really can see Liten Stein!" Malcolm commented and I thought that perhaps he was right.

In the other direction, the flatter, marshy part of the island where the ruined chapel stands had long shadows stretching across it from the uneven shapes of McGreggor Moor and the cairn on Frigg Moor. Over to the north, where the tiny community of Fremdes Haven was settled, the strange rock formations had just caught the sun on their higher pinnacles. My spirits were high. I think that I had stopped thinking about Elin for an hour or so.

"I hope Duncan hasn't gone back to sleep!" Malcolm commented, a propos nothing in particular, and I laughed.

"I don't think it would really matter if he has," I suggested. "He says he needs to revise, but he's worked much harder for these exams than I ever did – and they're only trials!"

"*Aja!*" Malcolm was chuckling. "But think what a disaster it would be if Alana did better than him!"

★★★

The little town of Storhaven was wide awake when we passed through it. We saw Jeannie sweeping the doorstep to her café, and down by the kirk the doctor, Emmylou, was deep in conversation with the nurse. They both waved, but were obviously not inclined to talk. We were tempted to stop at the bakery, the smell was so enticing, but in the end we just kept going, heading north on the track that leads to the cemetery, to Floirean's Cnoc, and eventually to St Matthew's Bay and the old airport. By the time we turned the corner and had our first view of the derelict buildings, the sun was higher and the shadows shorter, although our October sun is always quite low in the sky.

"It looks deserted," Malcolm commented, and I saw that he was right. There was no smoke issuing from the hole in the roof, no indications of any sort that anyone was around.

We tethered the ponies in our usual place and climbed down onto the lichen-covered stone flags.

"It's really deteriorated," I commented, looking around.

"*Aja.*" Malcolm was strolling over the broken concrete towards the beach. "I thought I'd heard that the sea had topped the sand dunes," he called over his shoulder. "Look – you can see where the water broke through!"

I walked over to join him. Malcolm was right. The first time we had visited St Matthew's Bay the dunes had been high and there had been marram grass growing in clumps on either side of the footpath that the refugees used to get to the beach. Now the gap was wider, more like a gully, with definite ripple marks of the receding sea on the wet sand.

"Freya Munro told me that Mirren wanted her son to do voluntary work reinforcing the dunes with rocks," I told my partner. "Apparently he declined!"

"I bet he did!" Malcolm was laughing. "Can you picture it?" He was following the breach in the dunes towards the sea. "But someone's been trying to do just that! Look – there weren't any rocks here last time we came, were there?"

To be honest, I couldn't remember. On the visit Malcolm was referring to, we had just been getting to know the refugees. When I looked back to that time, more than anything else I remembered Marigold as a wee bairn, confiding and ignorant, enthusing about beach-combing and fascinated by the ponies we had borrowed. *And now look at her!* I thought. *A bright, intelligent lassie well on her way to womanhood.*

But Malcolm was right. On the beach side of the dunes, someone had started to build a barrier of rocks.

"I don't think that would hold back a rough sea at high tide," I commented, and the picture suddenly flashed through my mind of myself battling rushing waves as I struggled to go for help, years ago, before the *harkrav* slavers had been brought down.

Malcolm was staring out to sea. "I think we'll soon find out!" he said.

I followed his gaze. Sure enough, on the eastern horizon dark clouds were beginning to gather.

"The storm's circling around," Malcolm said, looking worried. "The forecast said the weather would hit us from the west." Then he turned and looked directly at me. "Marie," he told me, "I have a bad feeling about this. If the sea breaks through again… Let's move the ponies to higher ground, shall we?"

We turned away from the shore and headed back to the ruined buildings and our ponies.

"It's clouding over in the west, too," I pointed out as I glanced up the steep grassy bank towards the track.

"Ain't a good idea to be 'ere," a new voice told us, and there, standing by our cart, was Jarvis.

"*Hei*, Jarvis!" Malcolm greeted him, as if we weren't surprised, as if he hadn't suddenly seemed to appear from nowhere. "It's Malcolm. And Marie."

"Yeah, I knows you," the man answered a little gruffly. "You 'as that ginger beard! Ain't like nobody else's. And Marie wears that green jacket, not like the one what she used to wear. And you's always together! 'Ow's your Duncan? And Marigold? I sees 'er at that kid's burial up on the 'ill. By little Lavender 'oo got swept out to sea."

"Marigold's doing really well," I told the man. "And Duncan's good too. How are you?"

"I's okay." Jarvis was non-committal. "But I tells you what: there's one 'eck of a storm coming and we needs to move them little 'orses. I'll show you where I goes…"

Malcolm winked at me, but he said to Jarvis, "You appeared just in time!"

We untied the ponies and followed Jarvis. He led us to the narrow gap between the buildings of the old airport and the steep bank that marked the beginning of the slope up to the higher moors, heading towards what had once been the runway, and then across the broken concrete to the northern end. At first, I couldn't see where we were heading but as we reached what must, at one point, have been a place where a small plane could turn, I saw that there was a track leading up towards higher land.

"Will them 'orses be all right?" Jarvis wondered. "They's small but they's pulling that cart and I ain't never brought no animals up 'ere before."

"They're used to hills and moors," Malcolm explained. "But if the going's too tight for them while they're still pulling the trap, we probably ought to take them out of their harnesses and lead them."

"Might not be necessary," Jarvis commented. "It ain't far. Only me and the sheeps comes 'ere normally."

The path didn't get more difficult to navigate. It was more than a sheep track, and our carts are always built to be long and narrow to cope with the tracks on the island. We followed Jarvis, who walked easily across the rough terrain and up the rocky track despite his bare feet, and then the path took a sharp turn and we found ourselves facing the entrance to a cave.

"Caves're all over the place 'ere," Jarvis commented as he led the way out of the watery sunlight into the cool, dark space. "But most of 'em faces the sea. This 'ere cave's the only one I seen what faces the sun at its 'ighest. I lives 'ere now."

We led the ponies and cart into Jarvis's new home. The entrance was relatively narrow but inside the space widened out and there was plenty of room to release and tether the ponies and park the cart out of the way. A small fire was smouldering within a ring of stones on the floor, and by the dim light we could see that Jarvis had moved his possessions from the derelict arrivals and departures hall into his new dwelling.

"I closes ever'fing up at night," he told us, almost proudly, and indicated a piece of corrugated metal leaning by the cave entrance. "Safer 'ere than down there, with prowlers and what 'ave you. They doesn't know what I's 'ere."

Malcolm had turned on the torch on his phone, and was looking around. "Did you level the floor and construct this storage?" he asked, pointing the light at what appeared to be shelves created by chipping out the rock. "How on earth did you manage it? Do you have tools?"

Jarvis was pouring water into a can that had once been a catering tin of tomatoes. "I's making tea!" he explained. Then, "No, I ain't done no building in 'ere. Them shelves was already there. Someone else been living 'ere, years ago, I fink. Before we was brought to this 'ere island. I used to 'ide in this cave before you lot freed us, when I wanted to get away from everyone. I 'ides in 'ere again now. It's good to 'ave somewhere to go in secret. I learnt that when I were a nipper."

Back in the ruined airport building the refugees had utilised anything they could find to make their lives comfortable – or at least, less uncomfortable than they would otherwise have been. I saw that Jarvis had moved many of the seat cushions on which he and his friends had slept, and made a bed of sorts along one side of the cave. Somehow, he had managed to prise away one bench seat (the sort that are usually anchored firmly to the floor) and had placed it close to the mouth of the cave. That was where Jarvis and I sat to drink the 'tea' that he offered us. Malcolm perched on a rock opposite.

When Jarvis had said that his cave entrance faced the sun at its highest, of course, he was telling us that it faced south. From where we were seated there wasn't actually much to see. To our right as we looked out, the hill rose steeply, covered in grass and, if I was not mistaken, blaeberry plants now past their fruiting time. We could see straight ahead, but only a few feet, and then there was a wall of rock, hiding the turn to the lower ground.

"This is a good hiding place," Malcolm commented. "Nobody would find you unless they were really looking."

"That's what I thinks," agreed Jarvis, gulping his scalding hot drink. "But it gets smoky if I closes up the door. And I 'as to, sometimes."

"*Aja*, it must get cold in here," I agreed, thinking of my warm bothy.

"Ain't just that!" the man told me. "I 'as to keep away from them uvvers. 'Out of sight, out of mind', that's what one of them foster carers used to say."

All the while we were talking, the light seemed to be dimming. Then I noticed that a breeze was catching at my hair.

Jarvis stood up and peered out. "'Ere it comes!" he warned us. And right at that moment we heard the crack and long-drawn-out rumble of thunder.

I don't know if it's because the climate has changed, or whether living so far north and in the middle of the Atlantic was the cause, but during my childhood in Melrose and my brief university career in Edinburgh I had never seen storms such as, by then, we experienced on En-Somi. It was suddenly dark. The small patch of sky that we could see seemed to be a black, churning cauldron of cloud with lightning flashing from one cloud to another and sparking down to the ground. The rain was torrential, sheeting down so that it felt as if we were sitting behind a waterfall. Further into the cave, our ponies moved restlessly, and Jarvis went into the back of his dwelling and moved a few things.

"It leaks over 'ere," he explained. "I gets a puddle in the back of the cave. Ain't a problem – the airport leaked too." Then he grinned at us; his face lit up by the fire. "I don't suppose as your 'ouse leaks, does it?"

Malcolm laughed out loud. It was not so much the comment as the way Jarvis had said it. "*Nei*," he chuckled. "Not any more. But the bothy I bought – the place where Elise and Harry live now – that definitely let in the rain when I first slept there. And the snow!"

Jarvis came back to the broken bench seat and we all stared out at the crashing storm.

"It'll be 'igh tide soon," commented Jarvis thoughtfully. "I thinks what the sea'll flood in. It's done it before. I's glad I found you. Wouldn't be a good fing to be out in this!"

"*Nei*," I agreed. "It really wouldn't. But Jarvis, that's partly why we came over to see you."

"What? To see if I were all right?" Again, the man looked amused.

"Well, *nei*," Malcolm chipped in. "We know you can look after yourself. But do you remember, you asked us to keep an eye on that wee lassie? The one you saw singing down by the summer harbour?"

"Oh, yeah." Was it my imagination or did a cautious expression appear on Jarvis's face? It was difficult to tell in such a dim light.

"She's missing," I said. "Nobody knows where she's gone. We wondered if you might have an idea? You seem to be aware of most things that happen on this island!"

Just then, there was a long, bright flash of lightning and a low grumble of thunder. A few small rocks rolled down the bank outside the cave's entrance. By the light of the storm, I could see that I was right – Jarvis looked wary, almost guarded.

"Run away, 'as she?" he asked in a surprisingly non-committal tone.

"Maybe," Malcolm answered.

For several minutes Jarvis said nothing. He stared out at the whirling darkness and moved his bare feet a little further into the cave to avoid them getting wet. Then, "When I were a nipper," he told us, "I ran away a lot. Well, you knows – not from my mum, but from all them foster carers. When a kid runs away, that kid don't want nobody to find 'em. That's why they's gone missing."

"But what if they need help?" I asked. "What if they're in difficulty?"

"If they needs 'elp," Jarvis answered obliquely, "they'll get it. But if they needs privacy, they 'as a right to that too."

"But –" I wanted to say, *Elin's just a child! She doesn't need privacy, she needs care!* Then Malcolm kicked my foot and I stopped.

"I'd be happy to think that any lost child would get help if they needed it," he said, as if he were completely satisfied with Jarvis's remarks.

"Yeah, well…" Our host was clearly not going to say anything more on the subject of missing bairns. "Does them little 'orses of yours need water?" he asked. "'Cause I 'as a sort of bucket what we could use."

CHAPTER 13

"It's like two storms 'ave met, right over'ead," Jarvis commented.

An hour or more must have passed. We had remained seated just inside the mouth of the cave where we were dry, and where we could see the dark clouds churning and boiling in the angry sky. The lightning flashed and sheeted, sparking down to landmarks we couldn't see from our enclosed space. And now there was a new sound, closer than the crash of breaking waves – a swish and a swirl of water closer to us, down at the bottom of the slope.

"The sea's broken through," Jarvis commented in a resigned voice. "I knewed it would this time."

"It's as well you moved up here," Malcolm answered. "I can't imagine sea levels rising enough to reach this cave – not in our lifetimes, anyhow!"

"I 'opes not." Jarvis didn't sound too worried. "If them waves started coming up 'ere," he added, "I'd just move to a 'igher cave. That's what them people in the olden days must 'ave done."

I was intrigued. "Do you think there were cave dwellers here, then? Some time in ancient history? Have you found evidence of them?"

"Don't know about no evidence," Jarvis answered. "Ain't been no scientists 'ere taking fingerprints or nofin'!"

Malcolm chuckled. "*Nei!* Not that sort of evidence!" he explained. "Not to discover if a crime has been committed! Marie means signs – signs of people living here long ago."

I could hear the smile in Jarvis's voice. "I only thinks of one thing if you says 'evidence'," he told us. "Cops and law courts and prisons. I doesn't think of no signs. But someone made them shelves," he nodded towards the side of the cave, "and them marks further in. And cut steps –" Suddenly, abruptly, he stopped.

"Are there caves with steps up to them?" Malcolm asked, his interest obviously sparked. "I grew up on En-Somi and I've never heard of that!"

"Oh well…" I saw in the dim light that Jarvis was looking down at his filthy feet. "Maybe there is and maybe there ain't. 'Ow would I know?"

★★★

By mid-afternoon, the storm had moved on. We could still see dark clouds to the north, but above us the sky was a washed-out blue. We shared our packed lunch with Jarvis, and then decided to go and inspect the damage.

The tide was going out again, and the sound of the waves breaking beyond the sand dunes was less ferocious. The rocky ground right outside the cave was solid and secure, but all sorts of debris had washed down onto the track after that, and we slipped and slithered back down to the level of the old airport. There was water everywhere and a lot of sand that had obviously been washed in. The gully between the dunes that we had noticed earlier that morning must have been two or three times wider, so that we could see the sea beyond it, grey and ominous, with white caps foaming way out in the ocean.

Jarvis stood and looked at it all. He bent down and picked up a piece of paper – the label from an old soup tin. "I needs to clear up inside the 'all," he told us. "I's bin trying to stop the sea from coming in, but as fast as I puts rocks there, them prowlers move 'em away. It's a losing battle. And if I don't clear out the 'all, there'll be rubbish everywhere, and that ain't right." He looked around, and walked through the muddy sand to a rag that was lying in a puddle. "It'll get washed out to sea and then come in on someone's beach somewhere," he said, scooping up the wet cloth. "Or poison the fish in the ocean."

"We could help you," Malcolm offered. "We've got time, haven't we?" He looked at me and I knew he wanted my agreement.

"Of course!" I responded. "As long as we're on our way by sunset, we're fine."

We spent the next hour or so on some pretty unpleasant work. When the refugees had been freed, they had left the derelict arrivals and departures hall in a mess, taking only what they wanted. There was all sorts of litter inside and some of it had already been washed out into the surrounding area. We collected a pile of old tins, soggy cigarette packets, food wrappings, bits of plastic, an old sock with a hole in it and something that looked like a checked tablecloth with a brown stain on one corner. The tins we bundled up in some rags to take back to Hus (we were skilled recyclers by then), and Jarvis said he'd bury the plastic and burn anything he could set light to.

"Can't do nofin' about that old building, though," he said, standing back and looking up at the broken roof of the derelict departures hall, where a piece of plastic sheeting – a temporary repair – was flapping loosely in the breeze. "I suppose what the sea and the waves'll sort it out, over time." He kicked at a loose piece of marram grass that must have been uprooted and washed inland by the waves a few hours earlier. "Or them prowlers will knock it down," he added as an afterthought.

"Prowlers?" asked Malcolm, wiping his muddy hands on his jeans. It was the second time Jarvis had mentioned these unwelcome visitors.

Jarvis gave Malcolm a sharp look. "Yeah, well – I means anyone what might 'appen to come over 'ere!"

"Oh, I see!" Malcolm acted as if Jarvis's answer made entire sense. "Well, Marie and I ought to be going. There'll be a hungry boy at home, waiting for us."

★★★

"Well, I like Jarvis!" Duncan announced.

We were having a late meal. It had seemed to take forever to get back to Hus and then down to my bothy. My son was waiting, potatoes peeled and cheese grated, and while we showered and changed, he made dinner – or I suppose it was supper by then. Now we were sitting round the fire eating from our laps.

"*Aja*," I agreed, "me too. But he doesn't give much away."

"He gives more away than he intends to," Malcolm suggested. "We learnt a few things he might not have meant us to discover, when you think about it."

"Like what?" Duncan had fetched the frying pan from the stove and was waving the spatula in the air. "Who wants the last of my famous cheesy potato?"

"Not me!" I was full, so Malcolm and Duncan shared it.

"Well," my partner answered, "for one thing, we know that Jarvis sees people down at St Matthew's Bay, people he calls 'prowlers'. And we know that they have vandalised his efforts at building a sort of sea defence."

"*Aja*," I agreed. "And he knows of other caves – caves that even you didn't know about, Malcolm, when you were growing up on that side of the island. Caves with steps up to them…"

Duncan put his empty plate on the floor and stretched his long legs out towards the welcoming glow of my range. "How could that be, Malcolm?" he wondered. "I mean, Alana, Andy, Marigold and I…" Then he gulped. He had almost forgotten that Andy was no longer with us. Bravely he continued. "We wander all over our side of En-Somi. If there were caves here, we'd know about them!"

"Well..." Malcolm was looking out at the darkness outside. "I didn't actually live by the sea. We were up on McGreggor Moor, remember. And that road out to the airport – well, there wasn't an airport then. It was just a track that led to the cemetery and the *harkrav* bothies in Floirean's Cnoc. As far as we knew, it didn't go any further."

I was intrigued. En-Somi is a small island. The idea that there could be one whole peninsula that was virtually unexplored seemed ludicrous.

Duncan was interested too. "But Malcolm," he wanted to know, "how did Holti get to his bothy? It's up on top of the cliffs beyond St Matthew's Bay! And the bothy that Shawn and his lot have renovated?"

"Oh, those *En-Som-in-Fedii* came over from Fremdes Haven," Malcolm explained. "Along the top of the cliffs, or via an old track that led almost to a sort of crossroads by that ruined chapel. Your mam and I, when we were coming to get help the night the slaves were finally freed, we came that way, more or less. It's the coast that's inaccessible. It's just steep cliffs."

"So, on the north-east, by the Stacks of Seamus, there's no access from the ocean?" I wanted to know.

"It's just cliffs and a jagged, rocky coastline," Malcolm explained. "I've seen it from the sea, lots of times. Sometimes, depending on the conditions, the ferry would come that way, but quite far out. Haven't you seen the Stacks when you've been coming home from Shetland, Duncan?"

"*Aja.*" Duncan was thoughtful. "But if nobody ever goes there, it would be a brilliant place to hide."

I realised he was thinking about Elin.

"Mm." Malcolm was not impressed. "I don't think it's so much that nobody chooses to go there, as that nobody *can* go there."

"Except that Jarvis seems to know about other caves – caves with steps up to them..." I pointed out.

"*Aja.*" Malcolm was looking thoughtful. "I wish that Jarvis would be more specific about the things he knows!" He was quiet for a moment. Then, "There's the question of his 'prowlers', too. People who destroy his attempts at keeping back the sea. Who would do that?"

"Aha!" Duncan rose to his feet and stretched. "The plot thickens!" he exclaimed. "Meanwhile, I'm going to bed. Sweet dreams, you two!"

★★★

When I went into the *fi'ilsted* a day or two later, Olaf was sitting by the fire on his own, a mug of tea in front of him, staring into the fire. I was expecting to see Sigrid there, but school had only just finished, so she could be a while yet.

"Can I join you?" I asked.

Olaf looked up at me and smiled – his old, less stressed smile of six months or so ago. "Marie!" he greeted me. "Just the person! Petter, could we have some more tea here? Marie, there's something I want to show you!" It was lovely to see the old man looking so much happier, and a little surprising. It was even more unexpected when he passed his mobile phone across to me – the phone he so rarely used. "Look at this!" he commanded, clicking on something.

It was a piece of video – not well recorded, as if the internet connection had been poor or the device that had been used was old. It was Elin, and she was performing a new song.

O little bird, O little bird,
Are you lost?
Are you alone? Are you in danger?
Storm-tossed?
Where is your nest?
Where can you rest?
O little bird, O little bird.

O little bird, O little bird,
Why are you here?
Where is your flock? Where is your home?
What do you fear?
Why did you fly?
Why do you cry?
O little bird, O little bird.

O little bird, O little bird,
What will you do?
Can you escape? Go far away?
Find somewhere new?
How will this end?
Have you no friend?
O little bird, O little bird.

O little bird, O little bird,
What happens now?
The winter comes, the rain beats down,
The sun is low.
Will you survive?
How will you live?
O little bird, O little bird.

O little bird, O little bird,
Say your goodbyes.
This life is short, and death is long –
A bird must fly.
Your broken heart
Must now depart,
O little bird, O little bird.

I didn't know what to say. Like so many of Elin's songs, it was full of grief and longing. The *langspil* accompaniment was simple, but her voice had a yearning tone, a sadness which we had heard in her song of mourning for Andy too.

Olaf took the phone back. "It's beautiful, isn't it?" he said. "She sent it to me this morning."

"*Aja*," I agreed. "It is lovely – but worrying."

"You mean because of the words?" Olaf asked, looking at the frozen picture of the lassie on the tiny screen and smiling.

"She sounds…" I wasn't sure how to put it. I wasn't even convinced I ought to say anything to upset Olaf, when he looked happier than I'd seen him for months.

But Olaf was no fool. "You think maybe she sounds as if she's leaving us for good?" he asked, with that kindly, wise expression I knew so well on his face. "And it does sound like that. But it won't happen. She'll be all right. She'll come through all this. I know that now."

"Olaf…" What could I say? How could he possibly be so sure?

He reached out and put one warm hand over mine. "I've been alive a long, long time," he told me. "I've seen things and understood things that not everyone is privileged to experience. And today, Marie, I *know* that Elin will be all right." He smiled into my doubting eyes. "And now I must visit the lassie's paps," he told me and, pocketing his phone, he reached for his stick. "There are more things in heaven and earth, Marie, than are dreamt of in your philosophy," he said, his eyes twinkling, as he left the *fi'ilsted*.

★★★

It had taken a ridiculously long time for members of the *Oyrod* to trace who owned the land where the airport had been built. The remaining *harkrav* members of the council seemed not to be in the least bit interested, although they might have had the connections to speed up the research. Malcolm found out quite easily that some sort of trust had taken over the area when the tourism project failed. It was called Atlantic and Nordic Holdings, but beyond that it was hard – for a while, impossible – to find any more details.

"At least one investor must be *En-Som-in-Fedi,* an islander," Malcolm pointed out. "Nobody can own land here without having island roots."

"But could they be people born here who now live somewhere else?" Duncan wondered. "Couldn't the Murrays own land here, even though right now they're on the mainland?"

"Oh, *aja,* absolutely. That's the problem," Malcolm explained. "All those *harkrav* who live on Floirean's Cnoc have the right to own their land, going back way into the mists of history. And so do their children and their children's children…"

"But isn't there some sort of central register of businesses?" I queried. "I'm sure I've heard of one. Companies House? Isn't that what it's called?"

"Well… *aja* and *nei,*" Malcolm answered unhelpfully. "It seems that Atlantic and Nordic Holdings is not a business but a sort of trust – we had that right – so there are privacy laws associated with their investments. We've got Patrick and Shona's laddie looking into it for us – he's training in company law, so he might be able to help. But so far, we've only been able to discover that there are six unnamed beneficiaries to the trust…"

Duncan had wrinkled up his nose. "I don't suppose it would help even if we knew that stuff," he pointed out. "Surely what we really need to know is who actually runs the trust? Aren't we hoping they'll help us reinforce the dunes?"

"That was the idea," Malcolm agreed. "Si thought it could become good arable land – but it might be too late now. The sea's broken through; the ground will be salty. It might just be better to leave St Matthew's Bay to the elements for the time being."

But an idea had occurred to me – or rather, a suspicion. "Actually, Malcolm," I pointed out, "the sea didn't really break through, did it? It was allowed through! What about Jarvis's prowlers? Do you suppose someone wants to hurt the beneficiaries of the Atlantic and Nordic Holdings people? Somebody had moved the rocks Jarvis had placed there, to try to prevent the erosion…"

"Anything's possible," Malcolm agreed, apparently unimpressed. "But it could just be kids from over in Storhaven, with nothing better to do than to make life hard for Jarvis. You know how some people are with those who are different!"

CHAPTER 14

Mid-October brought another huge storm. It barrelled in from the east carrying sleet in bitter winds, then whirled around and came back at us from the northwest. The older bairns finished their trial exams and the wee ones in Sigrid's school started to learn songs, those traditional songs that are usually sung around *Huldufolk* Day – telling tales of the antics of the hidden people. We had still discovered nothing about the whereabouts of Elin. Olaf had retained his calm assurance that all would be well. Elin's paps was keeping himself to himself. I saw him once, just outside the shop. He looked awful. *Another one experiencing the blasts of the terrible ones,* I thought.

Marigold and Duncan brought the two wee Stewarts down to our bothy one afternoon when school was over. Now that Thistle was mixing with other bairns in Hus, she had completely lost her English accent, and Alec imitated her as he tried out new words.

"Mam," Duncan said, "you ought to hear Alec sing! He's amazing!"

"*Aja!* You sing like a little bird, don't you, Alec?" Marigold addressed her brother. "Will you sing a song for Marie?"

"*Nei.*" The wee lad pouted. "Biscuit!"

"Biscuit, *please!*" prompted Marigold.

"He'll sing with me, won't you, Alec?" There were only a couple of years between Si and Rose's two younger ones, but since she had started school Thistle was very much the older sibling.

Alec looked uncertain. His eyes were still firmly fixed on the biscuit tin, which was on the counter out of reach. Then Thistle started to sing one of the songs she had been learning with Sigrid, and Duncan and Marigold joined in. They knew both the tune and the words from their years in the village school. For a moment, Alec just looked at them. Then, as if he had made up his mind, he joined in. He mangled the words a bit (well, he was only just three), but he held the tune perfectly. All the while he sang, he fixed his eyes on Thistle, following her lead. I had never heard a child sing with such a pure, clear voice.

When they had finished the song, wee Alec clapped. "I likes it!" he announced.

"I liked it too," I said. "You bairns sounded lovely. Have you been teaching him, Thistle?"

"*Nei*, 'Laf!" Alec corrected me.

I wasn't sure what he meant and looked at Marigold for clarification.

"Olaf heard him singing," she explained. "In the shop. So he brought his *langspil* to our bothy and started to teach him. Mam's really pleased. She says she's always wanted a musical child. And Paps says Alec must have got his voice from him, although I have my doubts! But Olaf said Alec's gift comes from the Spirit."

"Isn't he amazing, Mam?" Duncan sounded proud, as if Marigold's little brother was his too. "A real wee Stewart, that one!"

★★★

For the first time in a month, a ferry was due in. The message went around on social media and caused a lot of excitement. It was good news for all of us. There would be tins and packets of food that we couldn't produce for ourselves, chocolate and coffee, essentials like matches, books for the bairns and rechargeable batteries. There might be some mail, although most communication was online by then. Some more of Harry's apple trees were said to be arriving too. And going out when the ferry left would be half a dozen *gensii* knitted by our group and three hammocks knotted by Rose, fulfilling orders from Shetland.

"Could I take the cart over?" Duncan wondered, looking a little uncertainly at Malcolm. "Alana and Marigold would like to go to Storhaven, and we thought we'd offer Christian a lift too. His cousin lives over there, in Frigg Alley. We could see the ferry come in, and have lunch at Jeanie's…"

I knew why my son looked so unsure of himself. Malcolm had taught him to drive the ponies and had ridden alongside him often enough when Duncan took the reins, but my son had never taken the cart out on his own.

There was the briefest of pauses, then, "I don't see why not," my partner answered. "You could pack half a dozen of the beakers Si and I made. I promised Dougie and Ingrid they could have some. And maybe check with Tom whether the new chisels have arrived, although I'd be surprised. We only put the order in at the beginning of the month."

"Thanks, Malcolm!" Duncan grinned at my partner. "I'll look after the ponies, I promise!"

"I know you will." Malcolm patted my tall son on the shoulder once. "Your mam and I will be glad to be rid of you for a day!" he lied.

★★★

We had a lazy morning, pottering around the bothy and doing small jobs that we had put off. Duncan texted to say that they had arrived in Storhaven and that the ferry was delayed, but would be there by noon. Malcolm settled down to his computer over coffee, doing work for the *Oyrod* and (though he didn't admit it) playing a game or two. I was checking our accounts on my phone. The *gensii* had earned a good price and there were several more orders for Rose's hammocks. Christmas was coming and people everywhere knew what a bad idea it was to leave things to the last minute. Too many supply chains had broken down.

"Hey, Marie!" Malcolm suddenly exclaimed. "Listen to this!"

I logged off my account and gave him my attention.

"It's from Shona's son – you know, he was trying to find out more about that trust? The one which owns the land at St Matthew's Bay? Well, he's uncovered something interesting…"

I went across and looked over his shoulder at a document that was open on the screen.

"I thought this information ought to be in the public domain, if only we knew where to look," my partner told me. "And here it is. The trust was set up by – oh, Victor McLeod and Sons in Aberdeen, on behalf of Dominic and Poppy Fox-Drummin and Blair and Freya Munro. And the beneficiaries – well, of course! Two Fox-Drummins, two Munros, a Murray and a Williams!"

"Not them again!" I suppose I shouldn't have been surprised, but these were the very members of the *harkrav* who had been involved in modern-day slavery. Dominic Fox-Drummin had literally held me up at gun-point, and I had no doubt that he would have used his weapon, if events hadn't got the better of him.

Malcolm was skimming down a page full of legalese. "It's quite straightforward, actually," he told me. "Iona and I set up the same sort of arrangement for our bairns when she became ill – in case anything happened to me too. This was set up years ago… *aja*, here it is. Sixteen years ago." He looked up at me. "They were developing the land then, building the airport, buying up bothies for a song…"

"Hoping to make a killing," I said.

"*Aja*, and making sure their offspring got the benefit!"

My mind seemed to be unsettled, moving in several directions at once. The thought of Fox-Drummin and his rifle did that to me sometimes. "So, Magnus stands to gain from the trust?" I said.

"*Aja*, Magnus and his brother," Malcolm agreed.

"But the land's started to flood," I pointed out. "Will it have any value at all now?"

"I wonder..." Malcolm was frowning at his computer. "I think I need to do some more research..."

★★★

Of course, it was dark before the bairns arrived home. The sun must have set at around 4 o'clock, but the long dusk had started much earlier. Malcolm had just finished a long conversation with Shona's son, who was sure that the North Atlantic and Nordic Holdings trust was perfectly legal.

"The only thing he doesn't understand – and I don't either – is why it's all been kept a secret!"

"But has it?" I wondered. "I mean, when you and Iona created that trust for your bairns, how many people outside the family did you tell?"

"Well..." Malcolm was looking thoughtful. "Hardly anyone, actually. Of course, everyone knew we owned the flat and had a bank account, they just didn't necessarily know what provision we'd made for the bairns. That's a good point. There was no reason we should all have known about the *harkrav's* trust, but why keep their ownership of the land secret? When the question came up at the *Oyrod* meeting in the summer – do you remember? Si had said we could develop the land and we wondered who actually owned it. Well, there were several *harkrav* there. Surely one of them would have known?"

I saw what he meant. Then I remembered something else. "Malcolm," I asked, "can you think back to when Verity was still minister at the kirk and she invited us to a church council meeting?"

Malcolm grinned. "*Aja*, how could I forget? We sat at the side with Jeanie and she spoke so angrily about the refugees!"

"So she did!" I agreed. "But didn't the question of who owned the land come up then, too? And they were all there – Fox-Drummin and Fin Murray, and I think Blair Munro! And I think – but am I misremembering it? – that one of them said he had checked ready for the meeting. I can't remember who it was. But didn't one of them mention the North Atlantic and Nordic Holdings?"

"Oh!" Malcolm was impressed. "Goodness, it's years ago, but I think you're right. In fact, now that you've mentioned it, I'm sure you're right! So they owned the land all along, and didn't want us to know!"

"Because of the slaves," I suggested. "The refugees. The *harkrav* own land all over En-Somi, but that one piece of property – it would have tied them too closely to a scandal we were in danger of uncovering!"

"Which we *were* uncovering!" Malcolm agreed. Then he added almost gleefully, "What a thorn in the flesh we must have been!"

It was at that point that the bairns arrived. Actually, we heard them coming from the point where the shed was, where in those days we kept the cart. I had been expecting Duncan and maybe Marigold, but the other two bairns were there too.

Duncan ushered Christian and Alana in, saying as he took off his shoes, "Mam! Malcolm! Is it all right if Christian and Alana stay for dinner? Marigold's just stabling the ponies."

"Of course," I said, thinking how I would stretch our meal for two more hungry mouths.

Christian was a comparative stranger to our bothy. He had been there before, of course, but he was not a regular visitor. I saw how much he had grown. He was never going to be as tall as my Duncan, but he already stood head-to-head with Malcolm.

Marigold came in, her cheeks glowing and her eyes sparkling from the fresh air. She came across to me and gave me a quick hug. It was not unusual. Then she high-fived Malcolm and perched on the settle next to Christian. "So, guess who we saw in Storhaven?" she said. "Three guesses!"

"Tom, at the port?" I suggested.

"Jarvis?" Malcolm wondered. Then, "Not Elin! You didn't see Elin, did you?"

"*Nei! Nei*, we didn't see her," Marigold responded, looking penitent. "Sorry, I didn't mean to raise your hopes. But you weren't so far wrong."

"Her paps?" I was trying to think what he might have been doing over on the other side of the island.

"*Nei*. Magnus Munro was at the port, seeing his friend, that MacLoughlan guy, off on the ferry," Duncan told us.

"Did you speak to him?" I wanted to know.

"*Nei* – well… he spoke to us," Marigold told us. "We had just picked up the groceries – the cart was packed on the way home because we brought back stuff Robert couldn't carry, for the *fi'ilsted*. Oh, and Malcolm, we've got your chisels. Anyhow, we were just loading the stuff onto the cart and we saw Mirren talking to Magnus and his friend. She didn't look too happy. Then, when she'd moved on, Magnus came over to us."

Duncan was looking fierce. "I wanted to hit his smug face!" he grumbled. "I should have done!"

"*Nei*, you shouldn't!" Christian was always a peace-loving lad.

Marigold continued her story. "So he came up to us, and he said, 'Seems like the police are looking for that little friend of yours! Seems like everyone is!' And Duncan said –"

"It took the wind out of his sails, you could tell!" Christian interrupted.

"*Aja!* He did look taken aback," Marigold agreed. "Duncan said, 'That's because we love her.'"

"What a good response," approved Malcolm. "So, what was his answer to that?"

"Well, not very helpful." Duncan was looking grim again. "He just said, 'Better to have loved and lost...' and then walked away smirking."

"Mirren thinks he knows where she is – Elin, I mean," Marigold continued. "She saw us later, up at Jeannie's. She says he looked shifty when she asked him, and said it was none of his business. But the thing is, Magnus still isn't living at his mam's as far as she can tell. He headed off in the other direction when the ferry left. So, she's still thinking that Elin is with him."

The shutters started to rattle as the wind rose. The tide was in, and I could hear the steady roar and crash of waves against the newly-exposed rocks down on my beach.

"I'd just be glad to know that the bairn is inside, warm and well fed, at the moment," I said.

CHAPTER 15

H*uldufolk* Day was fast approaching, and the bairns were preparing for that, as well as for the Solstice celebrations. Duncan and Marigold made two wee houses for Alec and Thistle using wood from my beach and cardboard from the boxes our stores had arrived in.

"They're too good to destroy!" Malcolm exclaimed when he saw them.

"They'll be even better when the bairns have painted them," Duncan said. "We're going to take them up to Bothan Ros this afternoon."

"They've got to be burnt, though." Marigold looked serious. "You know as well as we do that if we upset the *huldufolk* there'll be trouble all year!"

I glanced at the lassie. Did she really believe our ancient myths? But *nei:* her eyes were twinkling in that mischievous way again.

"Well, we can't have that!" agreed Malcolm.

There was much scavenging on my beach, too. It has always been a good place to find stuff that has been carried by the sea from far and wide. Malcolm prized the wood, because other than the new apple saplings, there were no trees on En-Somi. We still found nylon rope, usually in bright, fluorescent colours, washed up on the shore. We had endless uses for that. Towns and cities on the eastern seaboard of the USA had flooded, and we discovered surprising treasures caught in the rocks: once it was a battered silver teapot (the sort that mint tea might be served in, in the Middle East) and on another occasion a tyre that looked as if it came from a tractor. It served as a swing in the open door of the school all one summer, and then Sigrid placed it flat on the ground, filled it with peat and grew alpine strawberries in it.

The bairns, of course, were interested in anything that would burn on our *Solstice-brennii* – the bonfires that would be lit all across the island on the shortest day of the year. They were good about checking with us, but they always looked a little disappointed if we chose to keep something. I remember when they found a piece of wood that looked like a large oak table leg and which Malcolm thought he and Si could use to create plates and beakers. He vetoed its destruction and the bairns acquiesced, but reluctantly. It would have burnt so well!

Nobody had forgotten Elin, of course. The general feeling was that she must still be somewhere on the island, for the very simple reason that she hadn't left on the ferry. There was a lot of sympathy for her paps and I'm sure that every parent of a lassie was profoundly grateful that it wasn't their daughter who was missing. Some of the population of Hus took their lead from Olaf. He seemed sure that things would turn out well, and although I couldn't see it, his attitude did seem somehow reassuring.

Lyle's parents came over from the tiny community of Fremdes Haven to see Joel, their oldest grandchild, present his first ever wee house to the *huldufolk*. It was a rather crooked affair, created partly by Lyle and partly by the laddie himself, and scribbled all over in red pen. The burning of the wee houses always took place down by the summer harbour – actually, it still does. Small groups of *En-Som-in-Fedii* walked an agreed and circuitous route joining several bothies, and demanding food for the *huldufolk* at each stop. I'm pretty sure that was the year that, for the first time, we located the fire on the black rock at the eastern side of the harbour – the old stone-paved quay was almost always under water by then.

I remember noticing that the crowd which gathered was larger than I had ever seen it. Holti and his permanent house guests, Quincy and Mo, were there, along with the people from Charlie's bothy. Those two households had trekked across the moors north of the *fjell*, coming down into the village past the Kullander's place. There were more wee ones too – Sigrid's three grandchildren were over from Storhaven and we had several young families in and around Hus. For the first time, the fire on which the wee houses were to be burnt had been built mostly by folk who had once been refugees on our island. It was, I thought, a good sign.

As darkness fell, the fire was lit. The bairns sang two or three of the songs they had learnt at school or at their own hearths and accompanied the melodies with the rather noisy improvised percussion that is traditionally carried on that day. We watched and applauded as the wee houses flared up when the flames reached them. Alec cried when his construction burnt, and Rose tried to comfort him by telling the laddie that he had brought good luck to the island. Joel was asleep on Lyle's shoulder and didn't see his creation burn at all. There was much laughter, and yet more food and drink were consumed. The waves rolled up the harbour, making white plumes as they met the rocks on either side, and frothing at our feet. The world seemed good, despite everything.

"What are you looking at, Olaf?" Harry had noticed that the old man had turned away from the fire, and was looking at his phone. The screen glowed bright in the darkness of the late dusk.

Olaf turned his head. "It's... it's just a message," he answered, and I thought his voice sounded a little shaky.

"Me see message!" demanded Alec.

I had a feeling Olaf needed his privacy. There was something about our old bard that suggested uncertainty.

"Me see!" Alec was tugging at Olaf's coat. "Me see!"

Si went over and picked up his wee son. "I know you likes phones," he told him, "but not everything on other people's screens is for little boys!"

"But it's music!" Alec was adamant. "'Laf, me hear music!"

Olaf turned back to face the rest of us. "Alec's right," he told us. "It is music. And I think it's a message for all of us." He held his phone out. "You all ought to hear this!"

Of course, it was Elin again. This time there was no video, just the sound of the bairn's sad voice.

Hidden folk, good folk, folk who keep us safe,
Little folk, friendly folk, folk who make us laugh,
Kindly folk, secret folk, gathered at our hearths,
Receive our gifts!

"She's written a song for the *huldufolk*!" Robert exclaimed.

"How lovely!" whispered Elise to Harris.

"Shh!" Malchi sounded stressed. "I want to hear it!"

The bairn had moved on to the chorus:

We don't see you, but you're there,
We don't know you, but you care!
We can't find you, you're everywhere!
Receive our gifts!

Coming here long ago, living on this land,
Small people, hidden people, ever-joyful band,
Watching us, guarding us, giving helping hand,
Receive our gifts!

We don't see you, but you're there,
We don't know you, but you care!
We can't find you, you're everywhere!
Receive our gifts!

Wise folk, gracious folk, spare us when we fall.
Gentle folk, ancient folk, hear us when we call!

Island folk, huldufolk, forgive us one and all,
And receive our gifts!

We don't see you, but you're there,
We don't know you, but you care!
We can't find you, you're everywhere!
Receive our gifts!

Village folk, friendly folk, folk who know me well,
Farming folk, fishing folk, hear me as I tell
Of lonely folk, of lost folk, of folk whose lives are hell,
And receive this gift!

There was a stunned silence when the song was finished. Then from the edge of the crowd came a sound that was part way between a groan and a sigh. It was Elin's paps.

"I let her down!" he said. "I failed her. From the time her mam died... My God! That my lassie should be one of the 'lost folk', or *'the folk whose lives are hell'.*"

Immediately he was surrounded by sympathetic friends.

"*Nei*, she's singing about everyone who isn't happy!"

"You've been a good paps to your young one!"

"It's a song, just a song!"

"She's just reminding us –"

Olaf broke through the group and put his hand on the man's shoulder. "She's doing what a bard does," he said. "She's not just singing about this day. She's singing about life!"

But I was worried. *Was* Elin singing about life? That last verse and chorus made me think more of death. Where was Elin? What was happening to that sweet lassie?

CHAPTER 16

Duncan and Alana both did well in their exams. Duncan was far better at Norwegian, but Alana scored the best physics result that her online tutor had ever seen. Marigold, in a lower year than those two, had also done well and had been asked if she wanted to join an extension class focusing on rural environmental sciences. Naturally, she leapt at the opportunity. Malcolm and I were a little worried because so much of the bairns' education was from books and videos. Malcolm's three youngsters, he remembered, did lots of practical, lab-based science, but of course there were no opportunities for that on En-Somi. At Duncan's request, both Malcolm and I on En-Somi, and Duncan's father, Bjorn, and his wife, Gudrun, in Norway, attended the virtual parent consultation interview, and we all agreed that considering the chaos that the world seemed to be falling into, we were more than happy with the education our lad was being offered.

Meanwhile, of course, the days were getting shorter and shorter. We left the bothy less than at other times of the year. Malcolm's little boat was upside down, high above the reach of even the roughest waves, and his oars were in our storeroom. I looked after my chickens, but they were laying less, and I embarked on a new knitting pattern, based on a traditional design but incorporating touches of my own, intended to be reminiscent of waves. The bairns were more relaxed now that their exams were over. They were helping others from the village to build the big Solstice bonfire on top of Fyrtarn Fjell, but also spending quite a lot of time in the meeting house, listening to music and talking about whatever teenagers talk about.

Our nearest neighbours, of course, were Elise and Harris. They lived in Malcolm's bothy; the one he had bought and renovated when he returned to the island. We didn't see a great deal of them although we were fond of the couple. They were unconventional folk and seemed drawn to others who were not in the typical *En-Som-in-Fedi* mould.

It was therefore neither a surprise nor a common occurrence when Elise arrived at our door one wet and windy morning. "Marie!" she called, opening the door a crack and looking in.

I remember I was sitting in one of our rocking chairs, some graph paper on a board, checking my new knitting design. "Hi, Elise!" I said, glad to be interrupted. "Coffee?"

So we sat in the friendly glow of the fire and chatted about this and that – nothing significant, as far as I can recall. Then, when she had declined a second serving, she told me why she had come.

"Marie," she asked, "you know Jarvis, don't you?"

"*Aja*, we do," I agreed. "Although, come to think of it, we haven't seen him for several weeks. We went over to the old airport in October, but since then..."

Elise looked thoughtful. "We haven't seen him either," she told me. "You know, Tom gave him that camera and I've been uploading his photos. They're really good –"

"I've seen them," I interrupted.

"*Aja*, well... The thing is, we never knew when he would call round; he'd just turn up and sit on that bench your Malcolm made out of slate, outside the bothy. He never would come in. But we haven't seen him for ages. And we heard from someone Harris knows over in Storhaven that the old airport has flooded. So we're worried..."

I felt a sort of vague anxiety in the pit of my stomach. "I'll make some calls," I said to Elise. "I'll let you know if we hear anything."

★★★

Neither Lyle nor Mirren had seen Jarvis in a while. Mirren had been over to St Matthew's Bay a month or so earlier, and confirmed that the ruined airport buildings seemed to be totally deserted.

"The tide was out," she told me over a slightly crackly line, "but there was wet sand everywhere; the sea is definitely reclaiming that area. It's a shame if that man, Si, from your side of the island is right and the soil was good. I didn't see anyone, but there were footprints inside and outside the ruins. And a big hole in the roof."

"Footprints?" I asked. "Or shoe prints?"

"Ah!" Mirren paused at the other end of the line. "Aye, I see what you mean. That man Jarvis is always barefoot, isn't he? These were shoe prints I saw – several, as if a couple of people had been there. Properly shod people."

Malcolm spoke to Tom at the ferry port. He had somehow got to know Jarvis a little, enough to discover his love of wildlife and to give him a camera. But Tom seemed not to have seen Jarvis either.

"The man's his own boss," declared Tom. "He'll show up when he's ready. I had an uncle like that once. He was in the Black Watch, and when he came out, he was – different. He used to wander around the Highlands. We never knew where he was, but every now and again, there he'd be, on the ferry to En-Somi, bringing us bairns gifts that were unlike anything anyone else ever gave us. We loved him. Jarvis reminds me of that uncle."

Holti, way over on the north-eastern peninsula, thought he might have seen Jarvis once, at a distance. "But it was a wild afternoon," the old man told us, "and the goats and I were having a difference of opinion about whether to stay outside, as they wanted, or to let me bring them in. By the time I had them safe and looked up again towards the clifftop, the man had gone. In fact, I'm not sure he was ever really there. The light was bad, and it was only a fleeting glance. I don't see as well as I used to…"

"Shall we go over there?" Malcolm asked me. "I'd be more comfortable if we knew for sure that Jarvis is okay."

"*Aja*," I agreed. "I think we should."

★★★

It was a grim day for travelling. I suppose it was the first week in December. The sun didn't rise until after nine in the morning, and it might not have bothered with the effort for all the difference it made. A thick, wet fog had descended on En-Somi, dulling the sound of the waves and the gulls. Even the ponies, who seemed always keen to be out, showed some reluctance as we harnessed them and led them up to the shed where we kept the cart.

Everything was muted by the weather. Even our voices, as we talked to each other, seemed muffled, and the sounds of the ponies' hoofs on the rocks had a slightly hollow ring. The village appeared like a shadow out of the mist and we didn't see anyone, although a dim light glowed in the shop. The wind turbines were absolutely still. A row of gulls sat on the arms of the newest of these elegant constructions; the one that fed electricity to the meeting house. They looked disconsolate, as if the fog was spoiling all their fun. Up on top of Fyrtarn there was a slight breeze, but it served only to make the mist swirl around us. We could hardly see three feet ahead of the ponies.

"I think we're in the cloud," Malcolm said, wiping the moisture off his face.

"A very cold cloud!" I complained. I had wrapped my scarf over my mouth and nose, but even so, when I breathed in, it felt as if I was living in a fridge.

By the time we reached Storhaven, the sky had cleared a bit. We could see a faint glow where the sun should be, but still everything seemed grey and brown and damp. We stopped off at

Jeannie's for coffee, had a word with Mirren who we saw outside the kirk, and then went on towards St Matthew's Bay.

It was just as Mirren had described it to me on the phone. The sand that had washed through the dunes was rippled and marked by the flow of seawater draining back out onto the beach. We walked through the gulley between the dunes, now a good three feet wide, and out onto what had once been a broad band of golden sand, a bay protected on either side by rocky cliffs. The beach had changed dramatically. At the exit from the place where the sea had broken through, where Jarvis had tried to build a wall of loose rocks, there was now a mound of sand, but around it was a channel still draining a small trickle of water back towards the ocean. The beach seemed smaller although the tide was low, and under the cliffs to the south where the refugees used to climb the hill to reach the next bay, the shore had been eroded completely. A steep rock face, maybe the height of a man, had been exposed.

"Nature is claiming her own," remarked Malcolm as we stood and looked at it all.

It was, of course, beautiful. Just at that moment, the low sun finally broke through the dissolving fog and shone brightly onto our faces. The wet rocks looked dark against the bluing sky, and the green of the cliffs higher up was vivid, as on a spring morning. The sea sparkled with a million reflections of sunlight, and the waves lapped lazily against the changed land.

We didn't find any footprints on the beach – not those of shoes nor of a man walking barefoot. It was as if no human had ever been there. Then we turned back and looked at the wrecked airport building. A good part of the roof had been torn off by the latest gale, and two breeze blocks had come loose at one corner of a wall and were lying on the ground. A heap of damp sand had washed up against a pile of loose and rusting metal, the only obvious sign that Jarvis had been trying to tidy the place up. There were no other remnants of the community that had lived there only four or five years earlier – no rags, no scraps of paper, no tins nor broken glass. Neither of us said anything.

Malcolm walked across and checked the ponies, then looked at his phone to find the time. "The tide'll turn in another hour," he commented. "Let's take these creatures to higher ground, just in case?"

Without discussing it, we turned towards the track that led behind the crumbling building and then up towards Jarvis's cave.

"If the sea completely reclaims this area," I pointed out to Malcolm, "Jarvis will only have access to his home at low tide!"

"*Nei*, I don't think there's any danger of that," my partner answered. "There'll be path down from the moors. Maybe the ponies couldn't make it that way, but I'm sure a man could."

★★★

The cave was empty, but reassuringly tidy. The fire in the stone circle had been banked down, glowing embers almost covered with layers of damp, steaming seaweed that would prevent the wood burning through too quickly. An old blanket was folded neatly on the cushions from the departure lounge seats that the refugees had prised free more than a decade earlier, and tins of food were lined up on the shelf chipped out by some other ancient inhabitant.

"I don't think anything's happened to Jarvis," I said, stating the obvious.

"*Nei*, I'm sure you're right."

"Should we leave him a note?" I wondered. "Tell him we called?"

"Can he read?" Malcolm countered. "I don't think we should assume anything. Remember, we had to teach Si and Rose…"

"Well then, leave him something? So that he'll know we've been here?"

"That's a good idea."

We looked at each other. What did we have that might serve the purpose?

"Oh, I know!" I exclaimed. I went outside the cave and looked around on the ground. I found a few small rocks and pebbles, and came back in. "He knows letters, even if he can't read," I reminded Malcolm. "Don't you remember? He put an 'L' on Lavender's grave!"

Malcolm grinned. "*Aja!*" he agreed. "So, two 'M's, for Malcolm and Marie?"

We left the sign just inside the entrance, reclaimed the ponies and cart, and set off back towards Storhaven. It had become a bright, clear day, more like April than December. When we reached Aeloff's Hill, we drove the ponies up the track as close to the cemetery as we could, then took out our packed lunch and climbed the last part of the way. We perched on the low wall, sideways to the sea, and Malcolm poured hot dandelion tea from the flask. You might think it was a bit gruesome, eating sandwiches among the graves of people we had lived with and loved, and our ancient forebears, but it seemed peaceful. If only we knew where Elin was!

★★★

Of course, it was a short day. At that time of year the sun sets early, soon after three. Already, by the time we had finished eating, it was low in the west, sinking behind the high moorland and the hills of Floirean's Cnoc. As often is the case, too, a breeze had got up as the tide came in. The waves at the foot of the cliff below the cemetery were noisier. We both put our jackets back on, grateful for their fleecy linings, and glad to find our gloves still stuffed into the pockets. Then, just as we were about to walk the short distance down to the ponies, we heard an unusual noise. Remember, there were then, as there are now, no forms of mechanical transport on the island. But we both knew what we were hearing. Somewhere there was a helicopter approaching En-Somi.

"There must have been an accident!" I exclaimed, my mind going at once to Duncan, to Marigold, to Elin. But we already had a very capable doctor on the island by then. Why call for help from Shetland? "It must be really serious!"

Malcolm looked tense too. He was staring out to sea, beyond the Stacks of Seamus from where the sound seemed to be coming. And then it appeared, shining in the afternoon sun, and definitely not an air ambulance – they are bright yellow. Nor was it a coastguard vehicle – they are red and white. This chopper was small, and was a shiny metallic blue with the letters 'PP' painted in gold on the side.

My partner visibly relaxed. "It's private," he told me. "Probably visitors for someone up on the Cnoc."

We both stood there, watching the helicopter approach. It flew almost directly over us, seeming to hover above our heads, and then, like a living creature, it moved a little inland, and we saw it settle on the moorland somewhere closer to Storhaven.

"Amazing technology," Malcolm said. "Somehow, I'm always surprised that they can be landed like that! Come on – we ought to head home."

I dare say we might have thought nothing further about it. It wasn't common even in those days for people to charter flights out to the island, but it did still happen. Elise's parents had arrived that way, and there'd been talk of Andy's siblings taking that route, although in the end they'd arrived on the ferry. I don't think we even talked about it as we drove the ponies along the broken and potholed track towards the wee town. But then, just as we passed the turning up to Freya Munro's bothy, we heard it again. You can't see her bothy from the track and, anyhow, we were in full shade from the moors and the *fjell*. We could, however, suddenly see the glare of lights and we could hear voices.

"Goodbye! Let me know when you get there!" And, coming clearly through the dusky air, "Give your father my regards!"

"That's Freya Munro!" I exclaimed. "I'd know that voice and accent anywhere!"

"*Aja.*" I could hear the serious note in Malcolm's voice. "And if that was Magnus she was saying farewell to, and I think it must have been, where is our Elin? Has she left with him?" He was very still, sitting on the bench seat next to me. Then he asked, "Marie, my love – do you think we've lost her?" His voice was full of sorrow.

CHAPTER 17

It wasn't to be expected that such a lovely, spring-like day would repeat itself. The next morning greeted us with cold drizzle and a gusty northerly wind. We had phoned Lyle when we'd arrived home the evening before and told him that we were pretty sure that Magnus had left the island.

Lyle sounded grim. Like us, I suppose he was wondering whether Elin had gone with him. Would we ever see the bairn again? How could such a sheltered lassie survive on the mainland, and with the sorts of people she would meet through Magnus? "I'll phone Mirren," he said. Then, "Thanks for letting me know… that poor wee girl…"

I was not surprised when Mirren arrived at our door later that day. It was mid-afternoon, and already dark and very cold outside. Duncan was lying on his bed, playing some sort of game on his tablet, and Malcolm and I were sitting by the fire. I was knitting, he was whittling. For centuries, I supposed, people had passed the cold winter months more or less like this, but without the technology and never in such comfort.

Mirren had adapted to En-Somi life with ease. Like a regular *En-Som-in-Fedi,* she knocked on the door and then opened it at once. "Afternoon, one and all!" she said. "Is it convenient for me to visit?"

Duncan, from his bed in the cupboard at the north end of the bothy, called out, "*Hei,* Mirren! How are the barbarians over on the east of the island?"

"Hi, Duncan," the *nasyoni* replied. "Barbaric as always, of course! How are the civilised folk of the west?"

"Tea?" offered Malcolm. "You look frozen! What're you doing over here at this time of day? Did you cross the pass on foot? In the dark?"

"*Nei, nei!*" Mirren laughed. "I came over earlier. Lyle and I had some paperwork to do. I'm staying at the *fi'ilsted* tonight – Malchi's roasting a chicken!"

Duncan padded over in his stockinged feet. He liked Mirren, I knew. It was something about the woman's calm cheerfulness and the way she spoke to everyone as an equal – even quite little bairns like Marigold's siblings.

"Lyle told me you saw Magnus Munro leave the island?" she checked, as she sipped her tea.

"Well, we heard him, to be exact," Malcolm corrected her. "It was dusk, but actually wherever the helicopter had landed on Floirean's Cnoc, we wouldn't have been able to see what was going on, even in broad daylight. Not from the track. But we heard Freya Munro saying her goodbyes to Magnus."

"Could it have been anyone else?" Mirren asked. "A house-guest of Freya's? You're sure it was Magnus?"

"Freya said, 'Give my regards to your father', so it had to be either Magnus or his older brother," I explained.

"I think I'd know if the older Munro son was on the island," the *nasyoni* said grimly. "He's the one who attacked Harris, isn't he? The nurse told me all about it. He's none too popular in Storhaven. I'm sure I would have heard if he had returned."

"We didn't hear Elin's voice at all," I said, bringing the subject back to what we had overheard. "And Freya didn't say anything to suggest that the bairn was there. But, on the other hand, there was nothing to indicate that she wasn't there…"

Mirren sighed. "Oh dear!" Then she perked up a bit. "Best-case scenario," she said, "Magnus has left, Elin is still here, and she comes home!"

But I felt less positive. So, it seemed, did Duncan.

"And worst-case scenario?" he asked.

None of us answered.

***

Mirren wanted me to go back to Storhaven with her, to try to talk to Freya Munro. She had never been particularly helpful to us, but we had to try. "You're the only person she even begins to talk to!" Mirren told me.

Malcolm drove us over. I am perfectly capable of managing a couple of ponies pulling a cart, but strictly speaking they were Malcolm's beasts and, anyhow, he hoped to meet up with his old friend, Dougie Fraser. At the last minute, Duncan and Marigold asked if they could come too, so with Mirren squeezed between Malcolm and me, the cart was rather full. The ponies, however, seemed unfazed by the weight, and trotted gamely over the pass as if they were not carrying five adult-sized people and battling a gale-force wind.

We'd set off in the dark that morning, wrapped snugly in our warmest clothes and equipped with hot drinks in flasks to sustain us on the way, but it was light by the time we reached Storhaven. The bairns had plans of their own, so we dropped them off at Jeannie's and Duncan drove Mirren and me to the turning up to Freya's bothy. We insisted we'd be happy to walk back, so he left us there and headed back into town, to The Castle.

Freya's bothy was lit up. The shutters to her east-facing windows were open and warm; golden light streamed out onto the patio area in front and onto the rather muddy track. We could see the woman sitting at her table, a laptop open in front of her, a cup of something by her right hand.

"Let me do the initial talking," Mirren told me. "This is *nasyonii* business, not a social call!"

I wouldn't say that Freya was surprised to see us. She looked us up and down as if inspecting us, but then opened the door wider to let us in. We both took off our boots. Again, Freya's expression suggested scorn.

"That's not really necessary," she said. "But if that's your custom... Please sit down. Why are you here this time?"

"We've just got a few questions," Mirren said. "One or two things we need to check with you."

"Well, of course," answered the woman. "I'll help you if I can, but I don't really mix with the sorts of people you deal with!"

Huh! I thought. *Your son is exactly the sort of people we deal with!* But I said nothing, and waited.

"Is Magnus around?" queried Mirren. "If he is, we'd like a word with him."

"You pick on my son!" exclaimed Freya, looking indignant. "No! He's not around! He's not even on the island any more!"

"Is that so?" wondered Mirren. "But he was here last weekend, drinking at The Viking's Rest. And there hasn't been a ferry since."

"Have you been following him?" Freya seemed full of rage. "He's old enough to drink in a pub, you know!" Then she took a deep breath, as if trying to calm herself. "In fact," she told us, "he left the day before yesterday. By helicopter. He's going to spend Christmas with his older brother."

"Ah! I see!" Mirren had at least got confirmation that we had heard correctly when we were driving past on our way home from St Matthew's Bay. It was a start. "Has he gone alone?" Mirren asked. "He hasn't taken any friends with him?"

"No, he has not!" Again, Freya looked angry. "His real friends don't live on this god-forsaken lump of rock! In fact, the so-called 'friends' he's made here have been nothing but trouble! Magnus is made for better things!"

"So, he went alone?" Mirren wanted to be absolutely clear.

"I've just told you!" Freya was furious: red in the face, eyes glaring.

"So, he didn't take Elin, his girlfriend?"

"She's not his girlfriend!" The woman stood up, walked over to the window, then came back. "Magnus has had nothing to do with her!"

Mirren glanced at me, and I took the cue.

"But she did leave her paps to come over to join Magnus, didn't she?" I stated it as if we knew it for a fact, although actually we were still not sure that such was the case.

Freya rose to the bait. "My son is an attractive boy!" she told us. "Of course she came over here to be with him! That doesn't mean he was interested in her – the little trollop!"

"But last time I was here," I reminded the woman, "you thought Magnus was seeing Elin. You said that any red-blooded boy –"

"I was speculating!" she interrupted. "You can't use that as any sort of evidence. We were just two mothers, comparing notes about our sons!"

"Why would we want evidence?" asked Mirren mildly. "Evidence of what?"

Freya spluttered. "Well, I… How would I know what that little slut has been up to?"

We were all quiet for a moment.

"The thing is…" Mirren took up the reins again. "That young girl is still missing. She came over here to be with your son, and now nobody knows where she is! And that's a bit of a problem for us, because she's only thirteen. If we were to discover that anyone had hurt her – in any way – well, that would not be something we could turn a blind eye to."

Freya Munro still looked very pink. "Don't be ridiculous!" she exclaimed. "Magnus wouldn't hurt a fly!"

But, I thought, *you know he would. After all, you more or less told me that he threatened you. And you're his mother. What might he do to a wee lassie?*

"Right!" Mirren sounded unconvinced. "Well, obviously

if Magnus isn't here, we can't speak to him. But you must understand: a missing child is a big issue. We'll need to contact the mainland police and ask them to have a word with him –"

"How dare you!" Freya was incandescent with rage. "I do *not* want the police calling at his brother's home causing a scandal. We've done our best, as parents, to separate our boy from a thoroughly delinquent girl. Now the rest is up to you. Find that chit and sort her out, and leave my family out of it!"

I admired Mirren's calm demeanour. She glanced at her phone – had she been recording the whole conversation? – and then said, "Well, Mrs Munro, I have just one last question. Do you know, or do you have any idea, where Elin might be now?"

"I do not know, I do not have any idea, and I don't care!" The woman rose to her feet and walked to the door. "I find the police work that's done on this island thoroughly unsatisfactory. You're biased against anyone who has money – anyone who's made a success of their life! It's time you opened your eyes. We're not the problem; you are!"

She held the door open as we put our boots back on. She couldn't wait to be rid of us.

"I'm sorry, Mirren," I said as we trudged down the track in the sleet. "I wasn't much help."

"Oh, I think you were!" Then she muttered, almost as if she were speaking to herself. "That boy's definitely done something he shouldn't! My only question now is: what is his crime? Is it to do with Elin or is there something else?"

"And the other question," I reminded her, "is still unanswered. Where is Elin?"

★★★

Between them, Mirren and Lyle had visited every bothy on En-Somi. Everyone knew that Elin was missing, but nobody seemed to know where she was. There was a lot of speculation, of course.

"Obviously, she left with Miserable Magnus!" Christian told us.

"She's in someone's storehouse somewhere, and they don't know!"

"She's being hidden by a friend because she doesn't want to come home."

"She's been abducted and now she's being kept in someone's cellar and used as a sex-slave!"

"She fell off a cliff –"

"*Nei*, she was *pushed* off a cliff!"

"She got washed out to sea…"

"She's dead!"

Any possibility might have been correct except the one about the cellar – none of our bothies have spaces below ground! Whoever offered that suggestion had been reading too many books or watching too many films.

Olaf was concerned. That last song, sent to him on *Huldufolk* Day, told us that the bairn was alive at that time and still had her phone, but it also suggested that she was in trouble. Our bard had a deep conviction that wee Elin would be all right, but his belief was being severely tested and a few of us wondered whether he had really 'seen' a happy ending to this awful situation, or whether his beliefs were no more than wishful thinking.

A group of us was sitting around three tables pulled together in the *fi'ilsted*. It wasn't a formal meeting; it was just that we all happened to be there at the same time. It was mid-morning and light, but in a dim, wintery sort of way, so that the fire in the hearth, the lamps, and the string of lights in the hammock hanging in the north-eastern corner, all cast a comforting glow and interesting shadows.

"You hear of it in cities," Malcolm said. "Bairns go missing and they're never heard of again, but how can it happen on En-Somi?"

"The Thames Valley Police visited the two Munro boys," Lyle told us. "They claimed to know nothing about Elin. The trouble is, the mainland police have so much to deal with now that one missing teenager isn't their priority. They logged a report, but that's it."

"And of course," I pointed out, "although we have our suspicions, we don't actually *know* that Magnus is responsible for the lassie's disappearance!"

"*Nei*," offered Petter, who was serving us coffee and muffins. "We don't *know* it, meaning we have no concrete proof, but don't we all believe it in our heart of hearts?"

"Magnus leaving like that is suspicious, though, isn't it?" Fiona was stirring her coffee, her brow furrowed.

"*Aja*, that's what I was thinking," Alf agreed.

"Maybe…" I thought we ought to keep open minds, although if I had been asked to bet, I would have put my money on Magnus Munro being involved in Elin's disappearance. "But it isn't *so* odd, is it, that the two Munro brothers should get together for Christmas? I mean, we know Freya can't manage Magnus, so sending him off to Oxfordshire or wherever – that would be a smart move on her part."

"Mirren's convinced the lad's done something amiss," Lyle told us. "She says she's got a feeling – a 'copper's hunch'. But of course, it might not be to do with Elin."

"Drugs, then?" I asked.

Lyle sighed. "The trouble is, those *harkrav* seem to know all sorts of ways of staying just within the letter of the law, while doing things that us folk – the *bondii* – deem immoral."

"Olaf seems certain that Elin's all right," Fiona reminded us.

"*Nei*." Alf was thoughtful. "It's not that, is it? He's sure she'll come out of this in one piece, but I don't think he believes all is well with her right now."

"Of course it isn't!" Fiona looked upset. "That last verse!"

There was a general murmur of agreement. Holti had sent Elin's song to everyone on our side of the island, because in it Elin seemed to say that it was a gift to us all.

"I agree." Petter had pulled up one of those little round stools. "'...*lonely folk, lost folk...*'" he quoted, then stopped, a catch in his voice.

"*Aja.*" Malcolm continued to recite the words of the bairn's song. "'...*lost and lonely, full of fear, full of sorrow, full of care!*'"

We were all silent.

"We hold her in the Light every evening," Lyle told us quietly. "Verity and I."

"We do too," Malcolm said. "How could we not?"

"So do the bairns," Petter told us. "When they're together in the meeting house after their classes." He looked at Malcolm and me. "Your Duncan started it."

"Bless them!" said Fiona. "They're good kids!" And I realised she was thinking of their Andy, perhaps remembering how Alana, Marigold and our Duncan used to visit their son.

Again, we were quiet. The fire crackled and beyond the *fi'ilsted,* the wind was whistling through the village, battering people's shutters, whirling their wind turbines. Malchi came out from the kitchen. He stood behind Petter and put a hand on his shoulder, and Petter briefly put one hand over Malchi's.

"We've been talking about Elin," he told his partner. "And thinking of Andy."

"*Aja,*" Malchi responded. "I thought maybe you were. I remember when we thought the morality police had got my sister... You can't think of anything else, can you?" It was common knowledge that in his youth Malchi's family had managed to escape a despotic, fundamentalist regime to come to the West. "You just need to have faith," Malchi added, his brown eyes looking sad, "and hope." And he went back into the kitchen.

★★★

Marigold and Duncan had started to read novels that had been written before the human race realised that we were heading for such a climate disaster: stories from way back in the early twentieth century. It had started with a set book in Marigold's literature class, I think, but both bairns were suddenly addicted to old-fashioned novels that dated from a safer time. They shared their excitement about H G Wells and George Orwell, and then Duncan discovered Sir Arthur Conan Doyle.

It must only have been a day or so after the conversation in the *fi'ilsted*. I remember that once again we were sitting in the bothy, all three of us engaged in our winter activities. It was, I recall, another dark, windy day. The clouds were low. When I went out to check on the chickens, I could only see a few hundred feet ahead of me. Everything was grey – the sea, the sky, the slates I was walking on. Only the surf and the gulls were white, and there was no colour.

"Hey! Listen to this!" Duncan had been lying on his bed, reading. He came over to the living area and looked at Malcolm's whittling. "Wow, pal!" He was impressed. "You're getting really good at that!" I had noticed that Duncan had called Malcolm 'pal' several times recently. It was, I thought, a term of affection. He didn't want to call him 'Paps' – he already had a father in Norway – but 'Malcolm' sometimes felt too formal. Then my son turned to the tablet he was holding. "This was a famous quotation once," he told us. "Listen! *'When you have eliminated the impossible, whatever remains, however improbable, must be the truth.'* Don't you think that's good? It's said by this old detective guy, Sherlock Holmes. Have you heard of those books?"

"*Aja!*" I think we were both amused, since that particular fictional character had been famous only a few years earlier, with films and television series made about him long after the original author had died.

"I've heard it said," said Malcolm, brushing wood shavings off his trousers, "that actually it's rather obvious."

"Well," Duncan considered that. "I suppose it is. But it's not what we're doing, is it?"

"What do you mean?" I was changing colours on my knitting, which has to be done very carefully if the fabric at the end isn't to look bumpy where the join is.

"Think about it!" Duncan sounded excited. "We've pretty much ruled out the impossible, haven't we? Or, at least, I think we have, as far as we can. We don't think Elin's left the island, and Mirren and Lyle have checked every bothy on En-Somi. That must mean that Elin is on the island, but not in a bothy. It seems unlikely, but if we've eliminated the impossible…"

Malcolm sighed. "*Nei*, Duncan," he corrected my son. "We haven't really eliminated anything, have we? We really don't know if Magnus took Elin off in that helicopter or if some *En-Som-in-Fedi* has chosen to keep Elin's presence a secret."

"*Nei*, but listen!" Duncan was frustrated. "So, okay, we haven't eliminated those possibilities, but we've exhausted them! Isn't that so? So, isn't it time we at least considered the improbable?" Then, sounding a little desperate, he added, "Elin must be somewhere!"

CHAPTER 18

Solstice came and went. Christmas came and went. Both were, I suppose, typical of celebrations on En-Somi. The day of the Solstice celebrations was bright and clear. I remember that Si and Rose brought their whole family up to the top of Fyrtarn Fjell for the first time; Thistle holding Marigold's hand and chattering away nineteen to the dozen, and Alec mostly carried by Si. Our fireworks frightened wee Alec. The banging and cracking was so close to him, and he hid his face in his paps' shoulder. But when the rising sun was seen by groups of *En-Som-in-Fedii* further away on lower hills or moorland, he loved them. Then, in his clear, piping voice, he insisted on singing a carol (which, I suppose, Olaf must have taught him) about a bairn who followed a star to a baby in a crib.

"He has a wonderful voice," Robert commented.

"I have heard," Freda Sinclair added, watching Rionnag and Thistle feeding each other oatcakes and giggling together, "that Olaf sang like that when he was a wee one. My *mori-mori* used to talk about him, when Mam and I visited her."

"Will he be the new bard, do you think?" wondered Paula Roberts. "I know Olaf is already teaching him..."

"Maybe," Freda agreed. "If Elin doesn't come back..."

Christmas, of course, is not a major celebration on En-Somi, although the arrival of the refugees among us had changed things a bit. Many of them had memories of Christmases back in England and, naturally enough, wanted their bairns to experience the magic they had known.

"Not me," Harry told us. "When I were a kid, it were all booze, booze, booze! I 'ated it. But Mandy (the woman he lived with) – she wants 'er kids to know about it, and 'er boy, 'e still remembers getting presents and that."

There wasn't another ferry due. The loss of the *Storm Warrior* as it ploughed through heavy seas towards the Faroes had made all the ferry companies cautious, so the community around Hus did what we could to create presents for the bairns. Duncan and Malcolm made several little recorder-like instruments, and although they were not at all tuneful, they turned out to be one of the most popular gifts – with the bairns, at any rate. Alana and Marigold cut up an old red felt blanket that had belonged to Alana as a wee one, and made tiny Santas, and Yanni somehow created toy boats out of scraps of wood left over from building the new bothy on Hunger Moor a few years earlier. I think one or two households killed a chicken – there were memories of turkey from back before they became refugees and then slaves – but most of us stuck with tradition and ate lamb.

Malcolm and I decided to have a Hogmanay party. Of course, we invited our nearest neighbours, Harris and Elise. Duncan wanted Marigold to come, so we invited that whole family, and we couldn't leave Verity and Lyle out. Then, at the last minute and without consulting me, Malcolm invited Olaf. I was, of course, delighted.

It was a lot of people to squeeze into our bothy. If it had been a less stormy night, no doubt people would have spilled out onto the slate area overlooking the sea, next to the site of another small bonfire built by the bairns, but it had turned bitterly cold and windy, with sleet turning to hail then back into freezing rain all evening. Duncan and Marigold solved part of the crowding problem by taking the wee bairns up onto our sleeping platform and telling them stories. Bonnie, who was a good sleeper, was settled on Duncan's bed, and the adults sat or stood where they could.

We ate cold lamb and pickles, and drank good whisky or dandelion tea, and at midnight we braved the bitter darkness, lit the fire (with some difficulty) and let off the few fireworks we had. We sang 'Auld Lang Syne', our tunefulness being much improved by the presence of Olaf and wee Alec; then those with bairns went out into the bleak night. Olaf had brought his *langspil* but, apart from that one song at midnight, he hadn't played it. Now, with most people away to their beds, he offered to play us 'a wee tune or two'. I remember that Elise and Harris were on the settle, cuddled up together, and Malcolm and Duncan were in the rocking chairs. Olaf liked to sit upright while he played, but I was on a cushion at Malcolm's feet.

It was one of those magical nights you think you will never forget. Olaf sang one song after another – sometimes in Scots-English, sometimes in our island dialect. Elise recorded some of it on her phone and sent it to her parents on the mainland to wish them a happy New Year. Duncan got up every now and again to top up people's glasses – alcohol for most of us, dandelion tea for Elise and Harris (they rarely drink anything stronger), and when the ballads had choruses we joined in, but quietly, so as not to spoil Olaf's performance. Then, at about two in the morning, while the wind howled around my bothy and the waves of the high tide crashed against the rocks on my beach, he started to sing a song that was almost new; a song that haunted us all. But this time it was different:

> *Hidden folk, good folk, folk who keep us safe,*
> *Little folk, friendly folk, folk who make us laugh,*
> *Kindly folk, secret folk, gathered at this hearth,*
> *Save our bairn!*
>
> *We don't see you, but you're there,*
> *We don't know you, but you care!*
> *We have searched, looked everywhere!*
> *Save our bairn!*

Coming here long ago, living on this land,
Small people, hidden people, ever-joyful band,
Watching us, guarding us, we need your helping hand.
Save our bairn!

We don't see you, but you're there,
We don't know you, but you care!
We have searched, looked everywhere
Save our bairn!

Wise folk, gracious folk, spare us when we fall.
Gentle folk, ancient folk, hear us when we call!
Island folk, huldufolk, please break down this wall
And save our bairn!

We don't see you, but you're there,
We don't know you, but you care!
We have searched, looked everywhere
Save our bairn!

We were all silent when he had finished. Duncan and Elise both had tears in their eyes – perhaps Olaf did too. My throat felt tight.

"Amen!" said Malcolm quietly. "Amen to that!"

With almost no further conversation, the party ended. Harry and Elise left holding hands, making footprints in what was part hail, part snow. Duncan shook hands, long and hard, with Olaf but neither said anything, then Duncan hugged us both – Malcolm and me – and went to his bed. Malcolm and I held each other close that night, not speaking, not sleeping for a long time.

It felt as if we were praying.

CHAPTER 19

The hail and sleet turned to snow – not mountains of the stuff, but enough to turn the world white and the paths and tracks slippery. Then it froze, and kept freezing. Climate sceptics huffed and puffed and made jokes about global warming. There were deaths in Canada, in America, in Russia, in China. Then there were fuel shortages on the mainland and all across Europe. "There's no wind; we're not making enough electricity!" wailed the politicians, ignoring the investments they hadn't made into storage. Then there were floods in the Sahara Desert.

On En-Somi, we were, of course, merely bystanders and distant observers to all of this chaos. It was indeed less windy than at times, but the air is very rarely really still so far out in the Atlantic, and if the arms of my wind turbine moved more slowly, and on occasion stopped altogether, it was only ever for a short while. Sigrid delayed reopening the school, not because of heating problems, but because the paths that some of the bairns walked each day were treacherous.

We had seals on our beach that winter. They like the open water better than lochs and harbours, and the sea below my bothy was rougher now that I'd suffered some erosion. Malcolm suggested that it proved there was an up-side to everything. Duncan took photos of the seals on his phone and sent them to his paps. The people of Norway, like us, were surviving the extreme cold well because they were prepared.

And we still didn't know what had become of Elin.

I saw Olaf standing outside the meeting house one mid-January afternoon. The wee ones had just finished school – classes had started again by then. The older bairns hadn't yet begun to gather, as was their habit at the end of the day. A lot of them had online classes until 4 in the afternoon. I saw one of those who had once been a refugee, Frankie, waiting to meet her grandchild, Shirley, and talking to Rose, who really didn't need to meet Thistle to walk a few hundred feet up the track to their bothy!

The old bard smiled at me. I felt that we were even closer since the Hogmanay party. We had all shared something special there; it had created a sort of bond.

"*Hei*, Marie," he greeted me. "Have you survived the Great Freeze?"

"*Aja.*" I grinned, walking over to him. "Have you?"

"As you see!" Olaf was also smiling, though there was an air of sadness about him too. There was always an air of sadness about Olaf at that time. "Elin's paps stayed with me," he added. "He hates to be on his own at the best of times, and when the weather's so bad…"

I wasn't sure what to say. It had occurred to me just a day or two earlier that we might never know what had happened to Elin. How do parents cope if their child is missing? How can anyone live with the not knowing?

Olaf was looking up at the *fjell*, which already loomed darkly against the faint pink and golden glow of the eastern sky; an echo of the sunset which was so bright on our side of the island. "That mountain casts a big shadow," he said, almost as if he were talking to himself. "It looks dark and dangerous, but behind it *bondii* are living their ordinary lives, looking forward to the spring…"

"You're thinking of Elin," I realised.

He sighed and turned back to me. "I'm always thinking of Elin," he told me. "I dream of the bairn. Sometimes I think these old eyes of mine have seen her in the distance. Or I've heard her singing…"

"You think she's out there, still?" I asked. "Even after all this time?"

The old man was silent for a while. Rose and wee Thistle greeted us as they walked to their bothy.

"Will you come and give Alec a lesson?" called out Thistle. "Paps is 'ere. Come and play for us!"

"I hope she's out there," answered Olaf, waving to wee Thistle but thinking of Elin. "I was so sure... I haven't heard from her since *Huldufolk* Day," he continued. "That's, what? Six weeks ago? And then it was only the song – no video. She could be anywhere." He paused, and I saw that the hand that was gripping his stick trembled. "She could be nowhere."

As he spoke that word 'nowhere', I suddenly felt a darkness, as if a huge wave was breaking over me – a wave of death. It was as if I was surrounded by something dark and cold; something hideous. The shock of it literally took my breath away and I gasped. In that moment, the most desperate words of all of Elin's songs came rushing into my mind all at once. From 'Hot, Hot Summer', I heard: *We are lying in our graves, you and me /the peat is over us, rocks below /short lives, but full /forever free.* I remembered from her song on *Huldufolk* Day: *Farming folk, fishing folk, hear me as I tell /of lonely folk, of lost folk, of folk whose lives are hell.* And perhaps most painfully of all, words from the song that Elin had sent to Olaf: *O little bird, O little bird / Say your goodbyes / This life is short, and death is long – /A bird must fly / Your broken heart /must now depart /O little bird, O little bird.* My mouth felt dry and my heart was hammering. For a second, I knew, just knew, that Elin was dead. In my mind, I saw her as clearly as I could see Olaf, with dark, stormy clouds behind her, jumping off a cliff.

Then the strangest thing happened. I cannot explain it – I have never really tried to. The words *the blast of the terrible ones* came into my head. Well, to be honest, it was more as if someone spoke them into the air around me; spoke them with such compassion that it was as if, instead of that ancient quotation, the voice had simply said, *All will be well.*

I didn't have time to think it before I said it. I don't know why I said it. Now, old lady that I have become, I am very sure of some things, and one of those is that there is a force of such love in the universe that we cannot begin to imagine it. But back then, I wasn't aware that I had many fixed certainties. I think I was as surprised as Olaf when I announced, with absolute certainty, "Olaf, Elin isn't dead!" Did I mean it literally? To be honest, I can't remember, although once I had said it, once the words were out of my mouth, a sort of conviction flowed through me. "She isn't dead!" I said again, this time feeling something new – a sort of joy.

"Well!" Olaf looked me directly in the eye. There was a time when he had been taller than me, but I think we were the same height by then. Old age had shrunk our bard. "Well!" he said again. "Marie, are you a seer?"

I remember that I felt slightly flustered; physically shaken. "I... *nei*, I'm no seer!" I insisted. "It's just that..."

"It's just that you know?" suggested Olaf, half-smiling.

I remember how confused I was. "*Aja*... well, that is, I haven't got any information. I don't know with my head! But..."

"But you know with your heart," Olaf finished. "Or maybe with your spirit? *Aja*, I know that feeling." He was positively grinning by then. "Hold on to that, Marie. I'm struggling to believe. Maybe it takes more than one of us. So, hold on."

★★★

I talked it over with Malcolm that evening.

"I just suddenly felt so certain!" I told him. "The way I'm certain that – oh, I don't know! The way I'm certain that I'm sitting here in our bothy on En-Somi!"

Malcolm didn't think I was mad. "I know what my son would say," he told me. "He'd say it was wishful thinking. That you want Elin to be alive. That your psyche can't cope with the idea of the bairn dead at the bottom of a cliff, or homeless on the streets of Glasgow. That's what Angus would say." He paused a moment. "He'd be wrong, of course," he continued. "I know you. You're not prone to that sort of psychological game. I could be. I think I could trick myself into thinking that something bad hadn't happened because I didn't want to believe it, but I don't think you could. You face facts. You always face facts!" He was quiet again for a moment. "No, whatever suddenly made you so certain while you were talking to Olaf, your mind wasn't playing games with you."

"So, what do you think happened?" I wondered. "How could I have been so sure?" Then I realised something. "Malcolm, I'm *still* sure! I really believe Elin's alive somewhere!"

Malcolm sighed. "Good," he said. "That's good! I wish I felt like that!"

★★★

The bairns were having a party in the meeting house. This was a new development. They had pretty much colonised that room for their after-school gatherings, but as far as I know they had all gone back to their various bothies in time for their evening meals. Parties weren't (and still aren't) really part of our culture, although feasts are. This party had been the idea of Alf and Fiona Kullander, although once the idea was put to Duncan, Marigold and Alana, they took over the organisation. It would have been Andy's birthday and the Kullanders wanted to mark it – but to mark it with joy.

I don't suppose it was at all like a party teenagers might have on the mainland. For one thing, their numbers were small. Even though they stretched the definition of 'teenager' to include Elise and Harris, and even though young Shawn came all the way across the island from his eastern bothy, there were still only twelve or so young people in all. They had decided against alcohol – Harris's influence, I suspect, and, anyhow, we have never served alcohol in the meeting house – but quite a feast was laid on. I believe Malchi created the first course and our bairns produced the cakes that served as desserts. Everyone still had sugar supplies back then, because the ferry had been in only a couple of months or so earlier, and I heard that good use was put to as much as they could lay their hands on! Petter invented a 'virgin cocktail', although I have no idea what he put in it. There was talk about asking Olaf to provide the music, but Alf had a playlist of Andy's favourite popular songs, so in the end they used that.

Malcolm and I, of course, heard all the plans but, old fogies that we were, we stayed at home by our fireside and didn't envy Duncan who was going out on such a bitter night. Once again, the temperatures were well below freezing, creating new meteorological records all across the northern hemisphere, and quite a degree of panic. I remember that we watched a film on Malcolm's tablet – it had a larger screen than mine – and I suppose we went to bed around ten.

"I used to hate it if one of my bairns was out after ten, in Edinburgh," my partner told me. "Of course, they were safe really – I taught them about never going anywhere alone, and they took taxis to get home, but you always worry. It feels different here."

"*Aja*," I sympathised. "I expect parents all over the world have a nagging anxiety if their bairns are out at night. The only worry I have is that Duncan might slip and fall. But he has his phone."

I think Malcolm was reading a novel on his tablet. I vaguely remember the thud as he dropped the device on the floorboards beside our mattress and started snoring. I was lying on my back, looking up at the sloping beams and the hammock Rose had made for us, and thinking I ought to sort through the things we were storing there, in case we had belongings that were no longer of any use to us but which others might like. I suppose I went to sleep wondering what exactly we had put in that hammock, because I know I was dreaming about sorting through a huge pile of clothes I hadn't seen in years. There was my school uniform from the days when I'd lived with my grandmother in Melrose, the pregnancy jeans with an elasticated waist that had caused such mirth when Bjorn saw them, and the red felt blanket which had been cut up to make Santas at Christmas. There was also a *gensi* belonging to Duncan which, in my dream, I had decided to give away, although my son wanted to keep it.

He was upset with me. "Mam! Mam!" My son was arguing, wanting me to change my mind about his favourite clothes.

"Go away!" I told him in my dream. "I've made up my mind!"

"Mam! Mam! Malcolm! Wake up!"

Someone had turned the light on. I felt Malcolm moving beside me, sitting up.

"What...?" He was as confused as me.

"Mam! Malcolm! Wake up! Mam! Malcolm!"

Now we were both wide awake. Suddenly, I realised: Duncan was standing at the foot of the ladder up to our sleeping platform, still wearing his heavy outdoor coat, snow melting on the shoulders and on his hair.

"What's the matter, Duncan? Is someone hurt?" There was Malcolm being annoyingly calm.

"*Aja! Nei!* Oh, I don't know! You need to come down here – quickly!"

Malcolm may have seemed calm, but he was down that ladder much more quickly than me; one hand on Duncan's shoulder, steadying my lad, who seemed to be panicking about something. I followed my partner down. The bothy door was still open and snow was landing on the slates, melting because of the underfloor heating. I went over to close the door.

"*Nei!*" Duncan looked distressed. "Jarvis is out there! Don't shut him out!"

"Of course not!" Malcolm walked over to the door. "Jarvis? Please come in. How can we help?"

Jarvis looked awful. The snow had settled on his hair and his shoulders; his feet were black and still bare despite the freezing weather. His long, dark coat seemed to have mud smeared down one side, and I thought his face was bruised. "I's dirty," Jarvis said, standing in the doorway. "And this ain't no social call."

"Fair enough." Malcolm was still calm. He had walked across to the kitchen area and was filling the kettle. "But there's no need to discuss the problem, whatever it is, outside. Come in! Shut the door! Let's not let all the heat out!"

My partner's apparent calmness was having the desired effect. Jarvis came in and closed the door, and Duncan slumped into one of the rocking chairs.

I was calming down too, taking my cue from Malcolm. "So, what's the problem?" I asked.

"The little puffling," Jarvis told us. "I can't reach her. I slipped; I thought I was a goner. She's on 'er own and it's wild out there, and I can't 'elp 'er no more! Them steps is broken! That poor kid is on 'er own!"

"Puffling?" I was, for the moment, confused. I knew that in the summer, during the breeding season, Jarvis had slept on top of the cliffs to protect the baby puffins from the gulls, but that was months ago. There would be no baby puffins around now...

Malcolm was in the act of pouring tea. Very carefully he put the pot down again, his eyes fixed on Jarvis. "Puffling?" he asked, sounding to me deliberately non-committal. "Do you mean Elin? Do you know where she is, Jarvis?" He paused, letting the man absorb the question. "Do you think she's in trouble?"

Jarvis was moving from one foot to the other. Vaguely, I thought that his feet might hurt as they thawed on our warm slates, but foremost in my mind were the questions Malcolm had just asked. Of course, Jarvis might well be referring to Elin when he talked of a puffling – a vulnerable little bird, needing protection.

"I bin looking after 'er," the man explained. "That little girl, she needed 'er privacy. I knewed what she were going through. I bin there myself. I's known lots of kids what needed to get away. 'Er was safe. I bin bringing 'er food and stuff what she needs. I wanted 'er to live in my cave, but she were frightened. She knew them prowlers. She fought what they would find 'er!"

Malcolm went back to pouring the tea. I saw him ladle spoons full of sugar into the mug he passed to Jarvis. "I see!" he said. Then, "Duncan, how are you involved in this?"

Duncan took the mug that my partner had passed to him. "I was just walking back from the party," he told us. "Jarvis was waiting for me by the shed where we keep the cart. He wanted me to come at once, didn't you, Jarvis? I thought – I wasn't quite sure what he was talking about, except that someone was in trouble. But I thought I ought to get you. You didn't want me to come here, did you, Jarvis? But..."

Jarvis was slurping his hot tea, still shuffling from dirty foot to dirty foot. "The tide's coming in," he said, as if that explained everything. "And a storm. There'll be big waves. 'Er's just a puffling..."

"Right!" Malcolm said. "Then I suppose we ought to see what we can do!"

"If we're going out in this weather," I suggested, now wide awake, "we need to be properly equipped. Duncan, I think your walking boots would be better than what you're wearing now. And you need a hat. Malcolm, have we got anything Jarvis can wear on his feet? Nobody ought to be out and about without some sort of footwear in this weather!"

Malcolm smiled at me across the bothy, with a look that said, *Well done! That's what the situation demands: practical common sense.*

"Oh, Mam!" Duncan looked so relieved. "Thank you! Yes,

I'll change my shoes. Malcolm, do you think Jarvis could wear your old boots? The ones Mam put in the hammock?"

I had gone back up to our sleeping platform, and was rooting out my warmest clothes. "Malcolm," I called, "should we contact someone? Lyle, maybe? Or the coastguard?"

"I'll leave a message for both *nasyonii*," Malcolm said, heading for the bathroom. "But we don't know yet what we'll find. We might not need assistance. Is your phone charged? Duncan, is yours?"

CHAPTER 20

We went out into pitch blackness. Malcolm was carrying a backpack. He had put in rope, a powerful torch, a first aid kit, and various other items we considered might be useful. Duncan had a couple of thermos flasks in his pack, plus chocolate from our storeroom and some bread and cheese. Jarvis was wearing a pair of socks belonging to Duncan and the boots we had put aside in case we ever needed them. He looked a bit uncomfortable and less sure-footed, but at least he wouldn't get frostbite. I carried a rolled-up sleeping bag. You never knew what you might need!

It wasn't actually snowing – not real snow. What fell from the sky into our faces, into our eyes, was more like tiny, sharp balls of frozen rain. The ground was slick with it; it beat like miniature drums on my waterproof hood and crunched under our feet.

"Where are we going, Jarvis?" Malcolm asked. So far he had led us on the track up towards the village.

"Over beyond," the man answered. "Where them caves is."

"What?" Duncan was keeping pace easily, striding along just behind Jarvis, in front of me and Malcolm. "Right over on the eastern peninsula?"

"Don't know about no… whatever that is!" I suppose Jarvis hadn't been brought up to know any topographical vocabulary! "Over beyond my 'ome," he told us. "Where them big towers of rock sticks up out of the sea."

"The Stacks of Seamus," I said.

"That's what I was thinking," Duncan agreed. "It's a long way from here. We've got to go into Storhaven and then out beyond St Matthew's Bay. Malcolm, should we go back and get the ponies?"

"No! Ain't no point!" Jarvis declared. "We don't need to follow no tracks. I knows a way across the moors! Follow me!"

It was a crazy walk. When we reached the village Jarvis didn't take us towards the pass, but north, and steeply up past the Kullander's place, which was totally in darkness, and then towards the little footpath to Fremdes Haven. We by-passed that tiny settlement too, still heading north-east. The ice continued to fall, stinging our faces, coating the ground with an almost luminous whiteness, but fortunately, conveniently, the moorland was frozen solid. I was fairly sure we were crossing old peat bogs. Walking that way in the summer would be difficult; would involve stepping carefully to avoid finding ourselves up to our knees in black, stagnant water. But that night we walked over the top of the marshland, the ice cracking under our feet.

"My feet 'urts!" complained Jarvis at one point. "Fink I'll take off these 'ere boots."

"Better not to," counselled Malcolm, and so we just kept going.

It was a wild night. The wind was gusting in one direction and then another, as if it were trying to find our weak points; the one part of each of us not protected by our jackets or hoods, or the scarves wrapped round our faces. Duncan somehow lost one glove. He knew at once that he had dropped it, but Jarvis was adamant that we not stop to find it.

"That puffling!" he urged us.

"I'll be okay," Duncan reassured us.

We could all hear the panic in Jarvis's voice. So we just kept going.

I had no idea how much time had passed; nor did I know where we were. The air was bitterly cold; it hurt my lungs to take deep breaths. Jarvis was driving us hard, striding ahead despite the alien sensation of wearing boots. Malcolm's powerful torch lit the few feet ahead of us, so that we seemed to be trudging through a small pocket of light in a black world. The sound of the waves became louder. Up until now it had seemed to come from our left, but now it seemed to be straight ahead – or maybe from our right.

"We're out beyond Holti's place," Malcolm said. "The Stacks of Seamus must be over there, maybe a little to the south of us."

"We's nearly there!" announced Jarvis. "You 'as to be very careful now!"

★★★

"Watch out!" Malcolm's hand was suddenly grabbing my jacket sleeve. "Marie, step back!" He was shouting against the crashing of waves far below and the howling of the wind. In the whirling darkness I hadn't realised how close to the cliff edge I had walked.

"Mam!" Duncan called, alarmed.

"It's all right," I shouted, although I knew I had been stupid. Jarvis had warned us to be careful.

"Where now?" Malcolm asked our guide. We were all shouting now. "Where's Elin?"

"'Er's down there," the man yelled, pointing to the cliff edge.

I could hear that quality of quiet that entered Malcolm's voice despite the fact that he had to raise it so much; that note of caution that spoke of dealing with a crisis. "Jarvis, did she fall?" he shouted.

"No! No!" Jarvis was frustrated that we hadn't grasped the situation. "'Er's in that cave, about 'alf-way down. Them steps led down to it, but they's gone! I can't reach 'er no more!"

Duncan was shining his torch at the ragged edge of the cliff. We could see why I hadn't realised how close I had got – there was a sort of break in the cliff; a chasm where there must have been some sort of rockfall. On either side there were another two or three feet of ice-covered ground, but in this one place there was a sudden drop.

"Did the steps go down there?" I shouted. I could feel the wind gusting around me, trying to knock me down, trying to tug me over the cliff edge. I took another step back.

"Yeah! Of course they did!" Jarvis was almost mad with frustration. "But they's gone! Look – there's the first one, but there ain't no more!"

Malcolm was pulling at my sleeve again, tapping on Duncan's shoulder, beckoning Jarvis. "Come back a bit!" he yelled. "We need to make a plan!"

The ground rose a bit towards the cliff edge. As we retreated, we were a little more sheltered. Malcolm squatted down and we all followed suit. Now, slightly protected from the tumult of the sea and the wind, we could hear each other without needing to shout so loudly.

"How long has she been down there?" Malcolm asked Jarvis.

"A few months," Jarvis answered.

"A few *months*?" Duncan was shocked.

Jarvis sounded, I thought, a little contrite. "'Er didn't want nobody to know!" he pointed out. "And I kept 'er safe! 'Er'd be safe now if them steps 'adn't fallen away!"

"Right!" Malcolm was only concerned with the present. "So when did this part of the cliff collapse?"

"When this ice started to fall," Jarvis said. "No – just before. I were away picking up supplies for 'er. That Jeanie, she sometimes gives me bread. 'Er don't know I's 'elping the puffling; 'er finks it's for me. But when I comes back, them steps 'ad gone."

I was thinking hard. Surely, if Elin had lived in a cave for months, it must be a reasonable shelter? "Should we wait 'till it's light?" I asked. "Then call the coastguards? They have all the equipment for winching Elin out."

Jarvis stood, almost dancing from one foot to the other. "No! No!" he shouted.

Malcolm stood too, put his hand reassuringly on Jarvis's shoulder, and soothed him. "All right!" he shouted. "Okay! Tell us why not!"

Both men squatted down again, a little out of the wind.

"The sea's coming up!" Jarvis said. "I called down to 'er when I got back. She said what the waves was coming into 'er cave. Ain't never done that before. 'Er were frightened. 'Er told me to go and get you, Marie." I could hear the hesitation in his voice. "And that little puffling, she ain't very well. 'Er's going to 'ave a baby." Then, more quietly so that we could only just hear his comment against the cacophony of the night, "Little puffling's too young to 'ave a baby!"

Malcolm had his phone out. The screen glowed in the dark and made his face look old. "We ought to call the *nasyonii*," he said. "Just to let them know what's happened." Then, "Bother! No signal!"

"Send a text!" Duncan advised. "If I text Shawn he gets it, even when I can't make a call."

Jarvis was impatient. "That little girl..." he reminded us.

"You're right!" Malcolm agreed. "Duncan, can you message as many people as possible? Jarvis, what's the safest way of making contact with Elin? How did you manage to shout down to her when you got back from Jeannie's?"

"You 'as to be right on the edge," Jarvis said, standing again. "But it weren't so windy then! I thinks what we might be blown over!"

"We'll have to crawl!" I suggested and, lying on my belly, I started to wriggle towards the place where the cliff had fallen.

"Mam, be careful!" Duncan called.

"Marie!" Malcolm stopped me. "At least let me rope you up before you try that!"

The freezing pellets of rain were still falling. Malcolm took his hands out of his gloves so that he had more dexterity when attaching the rope to me. *Thank goodness he knows what he's doing,* I thought. Then I was crawling forward again.

The last few feet to the clifftop were uphill. The ground underneath me felt solid, like rock, but then I put my right hand out and felt – space. I patted the ground to my left. It was still firm. I moved over a little to a more secure position, took a deep breath, and stuck my head out over the gap.

It was about the most frightening thing I have ever seen in my life. The drop below me looked sheer. Those cliffs are over a thousand feet high and I was peering down to the very bottom of them, where huge waves were crashing against rocks, sending up plumes of spray that must have reached thirty feet into the bitter air. I reached down into my zipped-up pocket to retrieve my phone and shone the torch down the cliff. About ten or twelve feet below me, I could see the steps Jarvis had referred to – or what was left of them.

"Elin!" I shouted as loudly as I could. "Elin, can you hear me?"

There was no answer.

"Elin! Elin!" We were so close. I didn't want to give up.

"Mam, come back!" Duncan sounded a bit frantic. "Be careful!"

I realised that someone had wriggled alongside me. "'Er won't be able to 'ear you wiv all this noise!" Jarvis shouted.

I tugged at the rope. It felt firm. I called back over my shoulder, "Have you got me, Malcolm, if I go over?"

"*Aja,*" he called back. "We both have – me and Duncan! Don't rush it!"

Even as I crept further forward towards that gaping space, as the crash and surge of the sea sounded even louder, as the wind caught my hood and blew it back onto my shoulders so that the frozen rain was beating on my bare neck – even while all that was happening, a tiny part of my brain was registering that Malcolm hadn't tried to stop me. He trusted me. Jarvis trusted me. Wee Elin trusted me enough that when she'd discovered her predicament, as the sea started to threaten her cave and there seemed to be no way out, she had asked Jarvis to fetch me. That separate part of my brain, the bit of me that was looking at the whole escapade from the outside, was amazed. What had I ever done to earn such faith? And I knew I couldn't let these people down.

I shone my phone torch over the edge again. The rock seemed to have split, the way a skilled person can split slate, so that there were lots of smooth, vertical flat surfaces. Here and there, though, it looked as if there were cracks where perhaps, if I was careful, I could put my feet. I slipped my phone back into my pocket and zipped it up. I realised how cold my hands were. Briefly I worried in case they might become numb; in case I couldn't hold on. It was a risk I'd have to take.

I shuffled round so that instead of my head being closest to the edge of the cliff, my feet pointed that way. I felt around with my boots, wriggled closer to the edge, felt the cold up-draught as my feet and legs stuck out over the edge.

Jarvis was still right next to me. "I fink you 'as to put your feet over a bit – yeah, like that. Then down. Yeah. A bit more the uvver way… no! Yeah! That's it!"

My right foot seemed to have found a crack in the rock. I tested it carefully. It was taking my weight. I could feel the rope against my belly; the roughness of it against my face. It was taut, holding me. I felt around with my left foot for another foothold, found one, descended a bit further. I was below the clifftop now, my face close against the sheer rock.

"You's doing well," encouraged Jarvis, leaning over the edge. I couldn't see him, couldn't look up or down, but I knew he was there: I felt his urgency.

What I thought must have been the remnants of the steps were to my left as I faced the dark rock face. I tried to use my left foot to find a better-placed foothold; a crevice that would take me in the right direction. At first, I seemed to find only smooth surfaces, but then – there it was! The ledge I needed! I tested it as before, to see if it would take my weight. It did. I shuffled across the rock face until both feet were secure on the narrow shelf.

"Elin!" I called. "Elin, are you there?" I hoped that now, since I was closer, she might hear me.

Suddenly, the lower half of me was covered in spray. An unusually large wave had crashed against the cliff, and I was drenched. Now, I knew, the rocks would be slippery. I was desperately holding on to something I had found sticking out from the cliff. I couldn't tell what it was. The root of some tough plant, exposed by the cliff fall? Would I dislodge it? I was certain that no climbing manual on earth would recommend that I cling to such a thing. I couldn't see where I was going. When I looked down, I could make no sense of the cliff face. All I could see was the swirling, churning foam far below. I was stuck.

How was it that, just at that moment, those words would come into my head? But they did. And although I had never deliberately learnt them, I remembered them exactly – the words Verity had recited when she was giving birth to Bonnie. The words that I had thought about so often since.

Thou hast been a strength to the poor, a strength to the needy in his distress, a refuge from the storm, a shadow from the heat, when the blast of the terrible ones is as a storm against the wall.

Malcolm had said that 'the terrible ones' were not people; they were moods, negative thoughts, voices in our heads that told us we couldn't achieve things. I dare say he was right. I had certainly thought so, until now. But I'll be honest with you. As I hung there against the sheer rock face, the wild ocean churning below me, the wind tugging at me, the hail beating down on me, I believed that the terrible ones were alive. For a few minutes then I didn't think of those things, the storm and the churning sea, as forces of nature. They *were* the terrible ones. They were out to get me, malevolent creatures, and I needed protection. I needed protection and I had it. My fear started to reduce. It wasn't that I stopped being scared; it was just that I was no longer frozen with fear. I felt again with my left foot, found another foothold, lost it, tried lower down, and found a solid, flat piece of rock at right angles to my part of the cliff. I shuffled left a bit more.

"Is you all right?" I could hear Jarvis shouting from above.

"*Aja!*" I called back, but I doubted if he could hear me.

I moved my left hand cautiously along the rock. I was still clinging precariously to the root with my right hand. Both feet were now on the new, narrow stone platform that my feet had found, so that my body was oddly contorted, flattened out against the surface of the cliff like a cartoon character. Then I found a firm, strong piece of rough stone jutting out, held on, let go of the root, and moved sideways again. I was standing upright on a ledge that was deep enough for my feet to fit squarely onto it. This was more than just a foothold. I still held firmly to my new rocky handle, but with my left hand I reached down, unzipped my pocket and took out my phone. I wanted to use the torch, I swiped the face of my mobile, still clinging on desperately to my rock, but nothing happened. I wondered if it was frozen or wet. I would have to use both hands. Did I dare? The rope was still taut, and I needed to see where I was. I let go of the rock and wobbled a little as a sideways gust of wind rushed up to meet me, carrying salty spray. I leant back a little. I was in a sort of corner now, slightly sheltered from the worst of the weather. I shook my phone helplessly, and at last the torch came on.

I was at the top of the remaining steps; the ones the storm and erosion hadn't destroyed. I could see them leading downwards, carved into the side of the cliff, following the shape of the rock round further towards the Stacks of Seamus – the south. There was nothing to hold on to. I don't have a bad head for heights, but I knew I couldn't walk down those steep steps in that storm, with the terrible ones blasting at me from every direction.

There was nothing for it. My Duncan, when he was a wee one, had never been acquainted with stairs since back then our bothy was all on one level. When we took him to Norway to see his grandparents for the first time and he was confronted with a staircase, he was lost. For the whole of that visit, he had navigated his way up and down between the two floors of the house on his bottom. I was about to follow his example.

I took a deep breath, felt for the second step, found it, stood on it, and sat on the top step. I felt the rope slacken a little – Malcolm and Duncan were giving me space to move, then it became taut again. I felt for the next step down, and moved again.

CHAPTER 21

Weeks later, I saw those steps from the sea, looking up at that steep, rocky surface, rocking wildly up and down in Tom's little rowing boat. If you didn't know they were there, you would never realise that a staircase had been carved out of the stone. Who had done it? How? But that night I was finding my way as much by touch as by sight. I think if I had been able to see the route I was taking I might never have attempted it.

It was like one of those nightmares where you keep doing the same things over and over again without achieving anything. The steps were uneven: some were narrower than others so that at times I was just perching on cramped shelves, and the distances down from one to the next varied. They followed the jagged shape of the cliff which jutted out into that swirling, crazy sea and the tumultuous air; I felt as if I was exposed to the elements more and more as I eased my way down, one precarious step at a time. At one point I was sitting on a narrow ridge of rock, facing directly out towards the ocean. The Stacks of Seamus were close, maybe two hundred feet away to the south: two huge chimneys of rock standing firm in the surging water. I was no longer frightened; I didn't have time. I explored again with my right foot and realised that these ancient steps were taking me around the side of the outcrop. I moved the other foot, found the ledge I needed, and shifted my weight, descending one more step.

I was looking down at a new gully now. The waves were surging up an ever-narrowing crevice below, and making a sort of *whoomph* noise as they met the sheer rock, sending spray up into my face. I realised that I had come down quite a distance. It had stopped hailing at last, but the wind was bitterly cold and I was wet through. The cliff face looked even darker than before; the rock beneath my hands and feet was slippery. I couldn't see where I was going.

"Elin! Elin!" I cried into the blustering wind. "Elin, are you there?"

And then – oh, what a miracle! Just below me, no more than ten feet away, I could see the vague, ghostly shape of a person.

The bairn was shouting, calling out to me, but I couldn't tell what she was saying.

"I came!" I shouted. "I came! Are you in your cave?"

The bairn called out again, asking me or telling me something, but I couldn't hear against the crash and *whoomph* of the breakers.

"I'm coming down!" I called, but I had no way of knowing if she had heard me.

I looked for the next step. Surely these stairs must lead directly to Elin's cave? The rope was taut. I tugged at it, trying to tell Malcolm and Duncan to give me more slack. Nothing happened; it stayed as tight as ever. I pulled at it again. Nothing. Was it caught on a rock? Had we run out of rope? There was no point in shouting. It was impossible that anyone up on the clifftop would hear me – even Elin, a few feet away, probably couldn't make out what I was saying. There was only one way to contact those above me. Perched uncomfortably, dangerously, on the slippery stone step that was as far as the rope would let me go, I unzipped my jacket pocket and pulled out my phone.

My phone had gone back into sleep mode. My hands were so cold, it was hard even to turn the device on. I fumbled with it, found the switch on the side, and the screen lit up. I found the app I usually used, tapped on it – and a huge spume of water rushed up to greet me: a fountain, a powerful jet of salt water. It knocked me backwards, flat against the rock. One foot slipped off the ledge below and, for a fraction of a second, I thought, *I'm falling!* but I braced myself, steadied myself, and realised I was still there, water dripping down my face. And my hands were empty. I had dropped my phone.

I took a deep breath. My heart was pounding and I was shaking from head to toe. What was I to do now? I tugged at the rope again. There was no give at all. I looked across to the place where I had seen Elin. She wasn't there any more. Had she gone back into her cave? Was I too late – had that last wave caught her, dragged her down to the churning water below, and the harsh rocks? Between the blackness, which I guessed must be the entrance to Elin's hiding place, and the exposed ledge where I was perching, there was a space of about ten feet. I assumed that if I could find them, the steps would take me to the bairn – if she was still there.

I gave one final tug at the rope. Still there was no slack, nor any answering tug. I took a deep breath. I would have to untie myself and travel those last, slippery steps unprotected. Unprotected? *Nei!* Once again, those words came to me: there was *a strength for the needy in his distress*. Well, I was needy all right! And, anyhow, what choice did I have? If I went back, what would happen to Elin? If I stayed where I was, wet and cold, wouldn't I die of exposure before morning? There was only one thing to do.

Clumsily, with difficulty, and with cold, numb fingers, I untied the knots Malcolm had tied so carefully. The sudden release of the rope felt strange. I saw the wind whip it away, up into the air, around the outcrop I had navigated with such difficulty. It had gone. Now it was up to me.

I can do this! I told myself. *The rope was only there just in case; I haven't actually needed it. I must have descended twenty steps – well, fifteen anyhow. It's only a few steps more…*

The waves were crashing into the gulley below, making that animal-like *whoomph* and sending spray high into the air. The water was dripping off me, running in rivulets over the step I was perched on. I couldn't see any sign of Elin. Shakily, I reached out and down with my left foot, found the next step, crept across the ledge I was sitting on, lowered myself down, sat, and reached out again. I had no sense of time. I had almost no sense of place. I certainly didn't picture myself wriggling across the almost-sheer surface of a hundred-foot cliff face in a storm. I thought only of where to put my foot next, how to lower myself without slipping. By now, when the sea heaved up in defiance of the rocks below, the water actually washed over my feet. The waves surged up, met me, soaked me, churned around me, sent up spray. I must still have been about twenty-five or thirty feet above the beach, but the tide was high and the waves were mammoth. I just kept going. If I thought of anything, it was Elin.

And then I was there – I was standing on the last step, seawater washing around my feet, the narrow cave entrance in front of me. Another huge plume of spray rose behind me, crashed down onto my ledge, and washed into the cave.

"Marie?" came a small, frightened voice. "Marie, is that you?"

It was, of course, still night-time – when Mo found my phone, broken and useless, on a beach a month or so later, it seemed that the clock on the screen had stopped at 5.15am. In the cave it was very dark, but Elin's pale face was just visible.

"Elin!" It was such a relief to see her.

She took two steps towards me, cried, "Oh, Marie!" and dived into my arms, just as she had all that time ago on Fyrtarn Fjell.

We clung to each other. I don't know which one of us was the most relieved to see the other. Behind us there was another *whoomph* and more water poured over the lip of the cave and flooded down the sloping floor.

"I can't live here any more!" the bairn sobbed. "Marie, what am I going to do?"

I looked around. It was hard to make any sense of my surroundings in the pitch black. I felt suddenly very wobbly, uncertain on my feet. "Is there anywhere we can sit down?" I wondered.

"Nowhere dry!" Elin gave a little sound: half giggle, half sob. "I've been sitting on these rocks..." She led me by the hand to a sort of stony bench. "But you'll get wet feet every time a wave comes in!"

"I've got wet feet already!" I reassured her. "There are worse things in the world!"

"*Aja!*" How could the bairn express such sadness in one small word?

We sat together, looking out towards the wild night. Fountains of spray splashed up, blew in through the cave mouth, and soaked our feet afresh as Elin had warned.

"You've chosen an unusual place to live," I said.

"Jarvis found it for me," the bairn told me. "He rescued me."

"He's a good man," I agreed. Then, "What did he need to rescue you from?"

Elin was quiet for a moment. "From Magnus," she said at last. "From his mam. From his paps, who wanted me taken off the island."

I didn't want to frighten the lassie by asking too many questions. Instead, I commented, "I wouldn't want to leave En-Somi."

More water splashed into the cave. A wave broke just below the rim of the entrance; a ripple of water flooded the floor.

"I didn't want to leave the island," the bairn told me after a minute or two. "But I didn't know how I could stay. And I had to hide from Magnus..."

"Why was Magnus such a threat?" I asked. Wee Elin seemed keen to talk.

"Because I'm pregnant," Elin told me. "I'm a minor and Magnus made me pregnant, and that would get him into trouble with the *nasyonii*, and then he couldn't go to university..."

"Well..." *So, Jarvis was right*, I was thinking. *She is expecting a baby!*

"He wanted me to have an abortion," she went on. "His mam said that if I had the baby taken out of me, and if I swore to secrecy, then they would give me some money and leave me alone. But otherwise..." She gave another sob and reached for my hand again.

"Otherwise, what?" I prompted her.

She seemed to hesitate. "I don't know. His paps is a powerful man, Magnus says. He always knows what to do. Magnus said if I didn't go along with what his family wanted, his paps would know how to deal with me. But I don't want an abortion, Marie!"

"I don't blame you," I said.

"Anyhow, it wasn't just that!" Now that the bairn had started talking, there was no stopping her, it seemed. "I know what he'd been doing, over at St Matthew's Bay. He didn't tell me, but I heard him talking to his brother on the phone. He thought I was asleep."

I held her hand tight to say, *I'm listening.*

"He broke down Jarvis's sea defences," she continued. "You know, he was carrying those huge rocks to the dunes, to make a sort of sea wall. It took him ages. Me and Magnus, when I first knew him, when he was still nice to me, we sat on the cliffs and watched him. And then, when the night came, Magnus took that horrible friend of his, the one whose parents sent him back to Shetland, and they moved the rocks and made a way for the sea to break through."

Was it my imagination, or had the tide turned? We could still see spumes of spray outside the cave as if we were sitting behind a waterfall, but no more water was coming in.

"Why would he do that?" I wondered.

Elin gave a little sarcastic laugh. "Money, of course!" she told me.

"But – isn't it their land? How would the Munros benefit from ruining their own land?"

Elin put her head wearily on my shoulder. "Oh, Marie!" she

told me. "I didn't know there were such horrible people in the world! I think they were going to get compensation. You know, from the government. Because prime agricultural land had been inundated by the sea."

"Prime agricultural land!" I was stunned. "It was a patch of concreted ground and a ruined building!"

"*Aja*," Elin agreed. "So it was. But who was going to come over to En-Somi to check? I heard Magnus's brother say that. All they needed were a few photographs. They took them on the beach, so that you could see how the waves had broken through but you couldn't see the old airport…"

We sat in silence while I thought about it all.

"So, Magnus and his friend were Jarvis's prowlers?" I said, checking the facts.

"*Aja*, and Jarvis knew that, but he didn't know why they were doing what they did. Until I told him."

"And Freya Munro, Magnus's mam, she knew you were pregnant?" I added.

"*Aja*. Not *was* pregnant!" Now there was a trace of pride in her voice. "I *am* pregnant! No Munro is going to tell me what to do!"

"Quite right!" I approved.

The tide was definitely going out. It was still dark, but on the eastern horizon the sky looked grey rather than black.

"But, Marie…" It was easier to talk now that the waves were making less noise, now that the wind seemed to be dropping. I could hear the uncertainty in the bairn's voice. "What am I going to do? I'm only thirteen. Am I old enough to be pregnant? Will the baby be all right? Will I be all right? Magnus said that if I went to term, the wee one would be deformed. He said it would be born with no nose, or with missing fingers. He said it might not have a proper brain. He said that's why there's a law about the age of consent. He said it was all my fault, that I should have known better." She was crying now, telling me all her worst fears, all the things she had bottled up for months. "Jarvis said that's a lie, but does Jarvis know? Was he just being kind? Sometimes I'm so frightened!"

"Jarvis is right, and Magnus was wrong!" I told the bairn, putting as much certainty into my voice as I could. "We'll have to look after you, and you'll have to be sensible, but we won't let any harm come to you – or the baby!" Could I promise such a thing? I had to.

Again, we were quiet for a while. The sky in the east was definitely getting brighter.

Then, "Oh, Marie!" the bairn said. "I wish I could go home!"

"Me too!" I responded. And I wondered how on earth we were going to achieve that.

★★★

The bairn slept, her head on my shoulder, my arm around her. Only a wee one could sleep like that, I thought: trusting an adult to sort everything out. I sat there in a sort of daze. Even though there was no immediate threat any more, my heart was pounding uncomfortably. There was less and less spray being flung into the cave, although the waves still sounded close. I could hear them crashing and surging below us.

I suddenly came to a while later. A gull was perched on a rock outside the cave, facing out to sea, calling to a mate. A second one joined it.

Elin stirred and lifted her head, releasing my stiff arm. "They nested there, I think," she told me. "They made ever such a racket! Jarvis and I, we had to be really careful as we came and went, not to upset them. Their chicks had already hatched when I moved in here, but the parents were still feeding them."

It was no longer pitch dark in the cave. The band of grey on the horizon was brighter – it was spreading upwards.

"We have beautiful sunrises," the bairn continued. "When I first came here, when the weather was good, the light shining in would wake me so early, and I would sit on that ledge in front of the cave and dream of what my life might be like. I used to pretend that Magnus would change his mind, and tell me he was really sorry for all the things he'd said and done. I used to imagine that his mam would give in and say, well, if we loved each other, it was only right that we should be together and raise our wee one together... I knew that wasn't going to happen, but I dreamed, you know?" She was quiet for a moment, looking out at the dark, churning sea. "But I couldn't write songs about it – about me and Magnus being together. I tried, but I just couldn't. And Jarvis said that was because they were hollow dreams."

What wisdom that man has! I thought, wondering how Jarvis could have understood Elin so well.

A rim of pure gold appeared on the horizon.

"Here it comes!" Elin sounded excited. She stood and walked over to the entrance of the cave, looking out. "Come and see, Marie!"

I joined her. The gold seemed to expand in front of our eyes, reaching upward, turning pink and red, and then the tip of the sun appeared, rose, and suddenly there was a path of shining, twinkling water from the rising sun directly across the ocean into Elin's cave. It was breathtaking. For a moment I forgot where I was, the predicament we were in, the troubles facing the lassie who was standing beside me. I was just there, the low sun dazzling my eyes, the utter beauty of the sunrise engulfing me.

Elin chuckled beside me. "That's how it made me feel," she told me. "Jarvis thinks the ancient people made steps to this cave because at some times of the year it exactly lines up with the rising sun. Jarvis – I'm not sure he ever went to school much, Marie. But he knows things."

"*Aja!*" I agreed. "He certainly does!"

Now I could see into the cave for the first time. It was quite deep, but low at the rear. As in Jarvis's new home, some previous inhabitant had chiselled away at the rock to make a sort of shelf, and I could see some of Elin's belongings, stored away from the wet floor. Her *langspil* was there, a small pile of clothes, her phone trailing its charger, and a couple of tins of the sort that biscuits come in at Solstice or Christmas.

"We ought to have breakfast," Elin instructed me, suddenly the hostess in her rocky home. She took one of the tins off the shelf, opened it, and brought out some bread. "I don't have much food left," she told me as she tore off a chunk and passed it to me. "This'll be a bit stale. Jarvis was going to bring me some more yesterday…"

I took the offering. I was, surprisingly, rather hungry. "He's looked after you well," I commented.

"*Aja*." The bairn giggled. "He calls me a puffling! And I am like a baby puffin, aren't I? Living in the cliffs, having to have my food brought to me!" Then she seemed to turn sad. "But I won't grow up and fly away!" she added.

I was thinking the same – not that Elin wouldn't grow up, but that, since we couldn't fly, I could see no way of getting out of the cave. The tide was still going out, but it wouldn't get much lower, and then it would come back in again. Either the wind had dropped or it had changed direction, but sooner or later there would be another storm – perhaps worse than last night's, perhaps later today. We needed to get out of that cave, back to the clifftop. We needed to be rescued.

"Does your phone work?" I asked Elin. It was a faint hope – Olaf hadn't heard from the bairn since *Huldufolk* Day, and presumably if she had been able to make a connection, she wouldn't have sent Jarvis all across En-Somi to fetch Malcolm and me.

"*Nei*," Elin sighed. "I tried, but even if I climbed up to the top of the cliff, the reception's really bad here, and Jarvis had to go over to Tom's to charge it. You know, Tom gave him that camera, and he charges that in Tom's bothy, but he had to hide the fact that he was charging a phone too. Everyone knows Jarvis doesn't have a phone! And, anyhow, I was worried Magnus's paps would find a way to trace my calls…"

"I don't think we need to worry about Magnus's paps!" I said, probably sounding rather grim. "But we do need to get back to the clifftop."

"*Aja*," Elin agreed. She was sitting in the mouth of the cave now, the low sun glinting on her pale hair, her feet resting on what was, in effect, the last of the steps before you reached the cave entrance – the threshold. "I don't know how we can do that."

I looked across at the back of the bairn, and I realised that she was no longer trying to help herself. And was it surprising after all she had been through? Jarvis, who had been her friend and protector for months, hadn't been able to help in this present crisis, but now she had an adult with her who, she believed, would know what to do. Like any young one, she was waiting for me to solve the problems we faced.

I went and sat beside her. Together, we looked out at the glorious view. Ahead of us, the sea was a bright blue, white caps rising and breaking as far out as we could see. To our right were the Stacks of Seamus, rearing up out of the churning water, their uneven surfaces dappled in sunlight. Below us and around the Stacks, the waves sucked and foamed, withdrew and advanced, splashed and reared up and rolled over. Gulls circled in the air, white against the blue sky. It was stunning – and wild. It was no place for humans.

I must admit, I was worried. Obviously, we had no way of contacting our friends on top of the cliffs. Malcolm and Duncan would have seen the rope fly loose; they knew I was no longer attached to it. Did they think I had fallen? If they tried to ring me, they would get no answer. My phone was in the sea or smashed to pieces on the rocks below. Only Jarvis even knew the location of this cave, and his way of reaching it no longer existed. Would they call the coastguard? If they did, would the coastguard come?

And then we both saw, at the same time, a sight to gladden our hearts. Way out in the ocean, beyond the threat of the churning, uncertain, treacherous waves around the Stacks, was a wee boat.

There were two people in it, rowing steadily north, getting closer and closer.

"They're looking for us!" I exclaimed. "Look!" I stood and started shouting. "We're here! We're here!"

Elin joined me, calling out, waving frantically. And they saw us. I don't suppose they heard us, but our movements attracted them. They waved back. They called out to us, and although we didn't know, we couldn't hear, what they were saying, still, we knew we were found.

After that, we just needed to wait. I had no idea what our friends would do, but I was certain they would find a way to free us. I could tell that the tide was turning again, and there was a steady, strengthening wind from the north, but although those were matters of concern, I was reassured.

★★★

It was Lyle who reached us at last. He abseiled down the cliff so that we first saw his feet, then his body, then his grinning face. "*Morgoni!*" he greeted us. "Fancy some coffee?" He was wearing bright orange gear, harnessed in a very professional-looking way, and with various bundles attached cleverly to him. He walked into the cave trailing rope, took out a device, and made contact with whoever he was working with. (It was Mirren, but we didn't know that until later.) "They're both here!" he said. Then, to us, "Are either of you injured?"

"*Nei!*" we both responded together.

"No need for medical help here," Lyle told his partner. "Emmylou doesn't need to come down – but we might need her assistance when we've brought them up." He turned his back to me. "Marie, can you unzip the compartment on the right? There's a thermos in there…"

After that, it was all business. The coffee was great – much sweeter than I would drink it at home, but just what I needed.

Elin looked a little hesitant. "Marie, is it all right...?"

I realised she was thinking of the baby. "Coffee won't do the wee one any harm," I encouraged her.

I saw Lyle give me a sharp look, one eyebrow raised, but he didn't comment. He just passed a mug of steaming liquid to Elin and watched in approval as she drank it.

Then came the tricky bits – and the frightening bits.

"Elin first?" Lyle suggested. A second harness had been lowered down to us. Lyle was talking all the while he was putting it on the bairn. "Now, all you need to do is do your best to climb upwards. You won't fall, we've got you, but try to stay as close to the rock face as you can. Think of it like crawling. If you swing away, you might get bruised, but if that does happen, don't worry. We'll have you, you won't fall." He was tightening straps, tugging at buckles, and all the while he was talking. "It's probably better if you don't look down," he instructed. "If you can, look up. You might not be able to hear me giving you instructions, but Mirren's up there, she'll tell you what to do. And Emmylou – the doctor – she's an experienced climber. Right! Now, the hardest part is going to be leaving the cave. Ready?" Lyle walked with Elin back to the entrance, showed her where to stand so that she could begin her climb, then called on his device, "Elin's coming up now!"

We both watched as she put her hands where Lyle instructed, lifted her first foot, climbed up beside the cave entrance, moved up again, and was out of sight.

Lyle turned back to me. "It could be much worse," he told me. "The cliff's steep but there're no overhangs. Abseiling down was pretty straightforward. She'll make it." He was looking round the cave. The floor had dried now, and the sun was streaming in. "Not a bad place for a person to hide in!" he commented.

"Huh! You should have seen it last night!" I told him.

"So, Marie, what's the story?" the *nasyoni* asked me, sounding serious. "You said the coffee wouldn't do the wee one any harm. Wee one?"

"*Aja*, I'm afraid so."

"That Magnus?"

I sighed. "*Aja*, Magnus Munro. And he's filled the bairn's head with all sorts of lies."

"Well," Lyle looked grim, but he sounded determined, "she won't need to worry about the Munros any more. Her own folk will look after her!"

"I wonder about her paps…" I didn't know the man well enough to know how he would deal with a pregnant thirteen-year-old daughter.

"Oh, no worries there!" Lyle reassured me. "He just wants the lassie home, safe and sound."

I wasn't so sure, but that was not the moment for further speculation.

Lyle's device coughed and then Mirren's voice called out, "Right, Lyle! One bairn safely delivered. Who's next?"

Down came the harness again, and once again Lyle was adjusting buckles, tugging at ropes, moving straps to make me more comfortable, and testing attachments. "You're good to go!" he told me. "Now, you saw how Elin left the cave? That's it. Good. No, I think it's easier if you move your right hand first. Yes… Good. Well done! I'll see you at the top!"

The sun was on my back, and the harness was warm and reasonably comfortable, although it pulled a bit under my arms. And no sooner was I away from the cave, climbing upwards, feeling all the while how someone on the clifftop was taking my weight, than I heard a welcome voice.

"Mam!"

I looked up. Duncan was peering over the edge of the cliff. I thought he was grinning.

"Mam," he called, "Malcolm says to hurry up! He wants his breakfast!"

I chuckled. How I loved them both!

EPILOGUE

We were going to have the thanksgiving in the meeting house, but it was another really hot day. People would be coming over from Storhaven to join the *En-Som-in-Fedii* from the west of the island, so plans were changed and instead we met on Fyrtarn Fjell, not far from the place where I had found Elin all those months earlier, and made some sort of connection with her.

Quite a few people from the little town of Storhaven came. Although it was true that Elin's paps had been overjoyed at the safe return of his wee lassie, he felt completely out of his depth dealing with a pregnant teenager. Malcolm, Duncan and I briefly discussed the possibility of inviting her to stay with us, but, to be honest, we didn't have the room. I know that Shona and Patrick at the shop had the same idea – and the same reservations.

The solution came from an unexpected quarter. Emmylou, our new doctor, was living in the flat that was once Verity's, over in Storhaven. It had three bedrooms – well, two and a box room! She offered Elin one of her rooms and said that Elin's paps could come over and stay whenever he chose. The disadvantage was, of course, that Elin was away from her friends, but the advantage was that she had medical help right there. I visited Elin quite a lot during her pregnancy – we all did – and I saw how the doctor looked after the bairn, made sure she ate well, learnt about what was going on in her body, got lots of exercise, and laughed a lot.

"I've never seen Elin so happy!" Duncan told me once, when he and Marigold had returned from one of their trips to Storhaven.

"*Aja!*" Marigold agreed. "But honestly, I'm glad it's not me! Emmylou says these last months are the hardest. I think if I ever have a family, I'm going to conceive late in the summer, so that my babies are all born in the spring, before the weather's too warm!"

"Well, that's what Elin did!" pointed out my son. "She wasn't to know that the first hot spell would come in May!"

Malcolm was laughing. "It's not always quite so easy to plan these things!" he remarked.

The baby was born on 21st June – the longest day of the year. A wee girl, small, but not dangerously so, and Elin came through it well, all things considered. They did a DNA test, of course, and so the *nasyonii* knew for sure who the father was, but Magnus never came back to the island. We heard that the Thames Valley Police were prosecuting, but I've never been certain about what happened. I suspect very little, because Elin wasn't asked to appear in court, although of course she gave a statement to Mirren.

We were spread out over the slope of the *fjell* where the little burn runs down towards Michaelmas Bay. Some of the younger bairns started damming the stream, which was a popular activity among the smaller ones that summer, and the rest of us spread out blankets and jackets and unpacked various treats. Malcolm had a cask of home-brew. Duncan and Alana were discussing universities – both were due to leave the island in time for their autumn terms. Marigold was sitting with Elin and Elin's paps, playing with the baby whose name would be announced for the first time that day, and making daisy chains.

Olaf gave the blessing – I suppose that's what it was. He leant heavily on his stick but he looked younger than he had done in the autumn. His joy at the return of Elin had been as great as anyone's, and greater than most. And he adored the youngest member of our community. "I feel like a *nas-motha-pari!*" he had told Malcolm happily, using the dialect for 'great-grandfather'.

He stood on a rock and banged his stick on the ground. Bit by bit, people stopped talking and returned to their families for the ceremony. The sun was shining, there was a gentle breeze, honey-bees were buzzing from moorland flower to moorland flower, sheep were baaing and, in the distance, waves were breaking.

"*En-Som-in-Fedii!*" the bard began. "We on this lonely island – we know about storms! We have seen troubles and heartache; we have known loss and grief. But on this hill," he pointed with his staff to the top of Fyrtarn Fjell, "up there, every Solstice, we remind ourselves that after winter comes the spring. After storms comes the sun. After grief comes rejoicing. We are here today to rejoice and to give thanks. Here is our Elin, who we feared was lost. Here is a bairn of our community, restored to us! And she has not returned alone. Let us give thanks for this new baby, Orani. Who knows what this wee one will see in her lifetime, but gathered here, we ask that she will know life and love, laughter and wisdom and song. As her mam will know! And her *pari-pari*."

"*Aja,*" people murmured.

"Bless her!"

"May she be kept safe!"

"Orani!" Duncan looked pleased. "It's dialect for 'song', isn't it? Andy would have loved it!"

"And now," Olaf said, "Elin and I have an offering for you."

Elin was smiling. She looked so young, and so happy. She handed the sleeping little one to her paps and took her *langspil* out of a bag. She and Olaf seated themselves on rocks, facing each other, and began to sing.

Blaeberry, bilberry, apple and kale,
Bless this babe.
Snow and wind and rain and hail,
Bless this babe.
Moor and fjell and hill and dale,
Bless this babe.
Make her one with you.

Make her wise, make her strong,
Wee Orani, mother's song,
Here among us she belongs,
We bless this babe!

Waves and sea and cliffs and rocks,
Bless this babe.
Goats in herds and sheep in flocks,
Bless this babe.
Clucking hens and crowing cocks,
Bless this babe.
Make her one with you.

Make her wise, make her strong,
Wee Orani, mother's song,
Here among us she belongs,
We bless this babe!

Peat and marshland, reeds and burn,
Bless this babe.
Dandelions and mountain fern,
Bless this babe.
Gull and orca, Arctic tern,
Bless this babe.
Make her one with you.

Make her wise, make her strong,
Wee Orani, mother's song,
Here among us she belongs,
We bless this babe!

Our En-Somi, lonely isle,
Bless this babe.
Old and young and growing child,
Bless this babe.
On this day and all the while,
Bless this babe.
Make her one with you.

Make her wise, make her strong,
Wee Orani, mother's song,
Here among us she belongs,
We bless this babe!

LOCAL DIALECT

Aja:	Yes
Amdatchi:	Silly, lacking in common sense
Bondi:	Peasant. Plural: *bondii*
Bothan Ros:	Rose Cottage
Brenni:	A ceremonial bonfire. Plural: *brennii*
Caldbrae:	Cold Hill (from 'Cauld Brae')
En-Somi:	Lonely Island
En-Som-in-Fedi:	An islander. Plural: *En-Som-in-Fedii*
Felbilli:	Common or cheap
Fi'ilsted:	Literally 'fish hearth', best translated as 'pub'. Plural: *fi'ilstedi*
Fjell:	In English 'fell'. A high and barren landscape feature
Gamla Husmannsplass:	'Old Homestead', the village
Gamla Hus:	Abbreviation of Gamla Husmannsplass
Gensi:	A pullover jumper. Plural: *gensii*
Goddi morgoni:	Good morning. Often abbreviated to *morgoni*
Harkrav:	From *har krav pa* – elites (literally 'entitled')
Hei:	Hi or hello
Huldufolk:	Elves (literally 'hidden people')
Hus:	Abbreviation of *Gamla Husmannsplass*
Huss:	The word for 'house' or 'building'. Plural: *hussi*
Langspil:	Zither-like musical instrument
Liten Stein:	Little Rock
Mam:	Mum

Morgoni:	Morning
Mori-mori:	Grandmother
Nas-motha-pari:	Great-grandfather
Nasyoni:	Police officer. Plural: *nasyonii*
Neeps:	Swedes
Nei:	No
Orani:	A song or hymn
Oyrod:	Island council. Members of the *Oyrod* and *Oyrodii*
Paps:	Father or dad
Pari-pari:	Grandfather
Solstice-brenni:	The fires lit to celebrate the Winter Solstice. Plural: *Solstice brennii*
Sommy klinger:	Corrupt and insulting form of *En-Som-fly-Kninger* or refugee

This book is printed on paper from sustainable sources managed under the Forest Stewardship Council (FSC) scheme.

It has been printed in the UK to reduce transportation miles and their impact upon the environment.

For every new title that Troubador publishes, we plant a tree to offset CO_2, partnering with the More Trees scheme.

For more about how Troubador offsets its environmental impact, see www.troubador.co.uk/sustainability-and-community